Charles Lambert is the author of several novels, short stories, and the memoir *With a Zero at its Heart*, which was voted one of *The Guardian* readers' Ten Best Books of the Year in 2014. In 2007, he won an O. Henry Award for his short story *The Scent of Cinnamon*. His first novel, *Little Monsters*, was longlisted for the 2010 International IMPAC Dublin Literary Award. Born in England, Charles Lambert has lived in central Italy since 1980.

# THE CHILDREN'S HOME

AARDVARK
BUREAU

# THE CHILDREN'S HOME

*- A Novel -*

CHARLES LAMBERT

Aardvark Bureau
London

An Aardvark Bureau Book
An imprint of Gallic Books

First published by Simon and Schuster Ltd, USA, 2016
Copyright © Charles Lambert, 2016

Charles Lambert has asserted his moral right to be identified as the
author of the work.

First published in Great Britain in 2016 by
Aardvark Bureau, 59 Ebury Street,
London, SW1W 0NZ

A CIP record for this book is available from the British Library
ISBN 978-1-910709-00-9

Printed in the UK by CPI (CR0 4YY)

2 4 6 8 10 9 7 5 3 1

ALSO BY CHARLES LAMBERT

*For Giuseppe*

# CHAPTER ONE

in which Morgan explains the living daylights
and the children begin to arrive

The children began to arrive soon after Engel came to the house. It was Engel who found the first one, an infant girl, in a basket, with a bundle of neatly folded, freshly washed clothes. The basket had been left on the steps leading up from the kitchen into the garden. Whoever had put it there must have known the way the house worked, because days might have passed before any of the other doors were opened; left anywhere else, the child would probably have died. As it was, no more than an hour or two had gone by but already the creature was blue with cold. Engel picked her up and held her, the small soft body pressed to her bosom, the small wrinkled face in the warm crook of her neck, for she didn't know how long; a living daylight was how she described it to Morgan when she brought the baby up to him in his study. Looking across from his reading with amusement, Morgan explained that the living daylights were always plural and that they were supposed to be the part of the human soul most susceptible to fear. She nodded, fervently, that's exactly right, it just goes on and on. That's exactly how it was, she said, with the child's small heart barely beating and the breath like a short hot knife blade on the skin of Engel's neck. Engel lifted the baby away from her body and held her out to Morgan, who shook his head.

She said they should tell someone perhaps, someone would know what to do with her, but Morgan disagreed. Left to himself he might have been tempted, what use did he have for a child, after all? But he could hear that Engel's heart wasn't in it. Just look at you both, he said. What could be better than this? Don't you know how to deal with her as well as anyone? Let her stay here with us, where she will be clothed and fed, and kept out of this wicked weather. At least for a while. Perhaps, he thought, the child's presence would encourage Engel not to go.

He held her later, when she'd been given milk and changed into fresh clothes from the bundle she'd arrived with; decent hand-sewn clothes, laundered and ironed, made of white cotton. He stroked the soft hair from the fine blue veins of her forehead, the first child he'd ever taken in his arms, and examined his feelings to see if they were altered in any way. He wanted to see if this child would change him; more than anything he wanted that. But what he felt seemed familiar to him; he had felt it before with small animals, kittens, a hamster he'd once been given, the little stagger of a newborn lamb; even with plants, those plants that flowered and had scent, that had touched his heart for a moment before they died. It will take time, he said to himself, only slightly disappointed. Miracles will take time. At least, in the meantime, the child might begin to love him. They called her Moira, which Morgan told Engel meant *fate*. At which information, Engel sniffed.

Engel watched the two of them, that morning, standing in the centre of the kitchen with a bowl of cream in her hand, which she was going to beat and pour on bread pudding for lunch. No waste was allowed in Engel's world; even week-old bread had its uses. The cream, the colour of old lace, came from one of the black-and-white cows that Morgan could see from his room at the top of the house, herds of cows grazing beyond the wall that encircled his own land, as far as the city itself, where his sister ran the factory.

Other children arrived soon after that, as though Morgan had earned them by taking the first one in. Some were abandoned, as Moira had been, left on the kitchen step, which was now checked hourly; others, he suspected, were given to Engel at the door, by whom, he didn't know. These were the children who arrived empty-handed. By the end of the third month of Moira's presence in the house, there were six or seven, he wasn't sure exactly, of varying ages. Moira remained the youngest. According to Engel, who seemed to know, she couldn't have been more than a few weeks old when she was left. The oldest among them was a fair-haired boy who walked into the house one day with a cardboard tag—the kind used for parcels—attached to his wrist, on which the name *David* had been written in a childish hand. Taken immediately to Morgan, he stood up like a little soldier before his desk, stared straight ahead, and announced, in a solemn yet singsong voice, that he was five years old and had no mother or father and would behave well if he was treated well. The ages of the others ranged between these two, Moira and David, whom Morgan regarded as the most precious, perhaps because they were the most easily distinguished; Moira, the first and youngest, and David, with his tag, the eldest.

Some of them came to the house in other ways. One morning, shortly after breakfast, Morgan was standing by the drawing room window and gazing out into the garden when a square of air above the lawn seemed to ripple as though it were silk and a knife had been drawn across it, and a child appeared on the lawn and began to walk towards the house, perfectly confident, it seemed, that she would be received. As she was. Later that day, when no one was likely to see him, Morgan went into the garden to try to find the place, standing on the lawn and testing the air with his hand for some point where its resistance might be weak, until he felt foolish and gave up. Walking back across the lawn, he saw that he had been watched by David, who was standing at the window directly above the drawing room. He waved, and was pleased to see David wave back. Like David, the new girl had a cardboard tag attached to her wrist, which told them her name was Melissa. She looked around the main hall of the house with a contented expression, smiling at David when he came to take her hand and show her the house, although she smiled at Moira in much the same way, and at the other children too; she smiled at everyone as though she had known and loved them all her life. When she saw Morgan for the first time, as he hurried through from the drawing room to greet her, calling to Engel as he did so, she ran across and hugged his knees.

Each day, Morgan would watch them eat, while Engel doled out food into their bowls. David and the second eldest, a girl with sad blue eyes and a missing milk tooth at the front of her mouth, whose name—because Engel had insisted—was Daisy, sat near the fireplace at a small wooden table Morgan had never seen before, which must have been acquired by Engel in the town and been when he was in another part of the house, or still asleep one morning. So much went on in the house of which he was unaware. The running of the place, he often thought, was blessedly arranged behind his back. The others were seated in a semicircle of high chairs, also new. Melissa and David and Jack and Moira and Daisy and Christopher and Ruth, each one as like and unlike the others as children always are. Morgan was proud to see his kitchen busy with these small, contentedly eating creatures, with Engel filling their bowls and spooning the food into the younger ones' mouths.

One day, in an effort to belong more intimately, Morgan dipped his finger into a bowl and licked off the pap, a sort of purée, as far as he could tell, of meat and cabbage. He was surprised to find it so good. I should like some of this, he said to Engel, who growled at him and shook her head. This is no food for you, she said. You're a big enough baby as it is. Later that day, standing in his bedroom, he couldn't explain to himself how deeply the manner of this refusal had touched him. He found himself weeping for the first time since the accident. Later still that same day, when he had thought he was alone in his room, he opened his eyes and saw two children, a boy and a girl, standing before him, dressed identically in striped smocks that came almost to their feet and thin white shoes, as soft and defenceless as slippers. They spoke together. Our names are Georgie and Georgina, they said. Hello, Georgie and Georgina, Morgan said, with some difficulty, the soft gs clinging to the surface of his tongue. Hello, Morgan, they said. So they'd already been told his name.

Mealtime with the children became a fixed point in

...tastes of the food that Engel ...rned her back, which she may ...e; his finger was constantly wet to ...m. The children had learned that when ...ere they should be quiet and eat their food, ... child was ever punished, certainly not in front of ... At times he wondered if Engel chastised them when he was somewhere else. He didn't think so. Did it occur to him that a child that never needed to be chastised was hardly a child at all, but a sort of living doll, or automaton? Of course it did. He knew there was a mystery about these children, and not only in the nature of their arrival, but he pushed the thought aside. In any case, the notion that Engel might do more than raise her voice, might use some sort of violence against them, could not be conceived.

The room in which Morgan passed the better part of his days was lined with darkly polished wooden shelves, and had no natural light. Each shelf was tightly packed with stacks of books of all shapes and sizes, reaching to the high panelled ceiling. The entrance was concealed behind a small hinged bookcase filled with dummy books, one of which—a collection of essays by an eighteenth-century cleric—acted as a hidden clasp. Even the two long windows that had once overlooked the lawns had been sealed to make more room for shelves, thought Morgan, absurd as this was in a house with dozens of empty rooms that might have held any number of books. What he didn't say—perhaps because no one had ever asked him—was that in rooms without access to natural light, there could be no day or night. In this room, known as the book room to distinguish it from the house's true library, which was downstairs, time was an uninflected, unending ribbon, an ouroboros. Morgan had arranged for a desk to be placed in the centre and, behind it, the swivel chair his father had used when he worked as a lawyer in the city. This was the room in which he read and, sometimes, before the children arrived and for some time after, wrote. The children were only permitted to enter accompanied, although they were always there for him in a way. He would feel their presence whatever he was doing.

# CHAPTER TWO

in which Engel chooses a room

Engel had been sent to him by his sister, Rebecca, he was certain of that. She came with several references that made no comment at all about anything she had done, but spoke highly of her character, as though it was her character that was on offer and not her skills. He was certain Engel had come from his sister because she knew so many things about him. She didn't say, in so many words: I know you like your bed linen to be folded back at an angle. I know you like your eggs to be scrambled with too much butter in a small copper pan and taken off the heat a moment too soon and left to almost set. I know you have nightmares and can only be soothed by a cool cloth on your forehead and no words spoken because words only make it worse. She didn't say these things; she did them.

The first time he noticed how much she knew about him, he was apprehensive. He would have asked her where she had learned his needs so precisely, but something about her no-nonsense manner dissuaded him. Then, by degrees, he grew used to it, and to her. Before too many weeks had passed, it was natural that she should perform these duties as a sister might. It hurt him a little that his sister should have chosen not to perform them herself, preferring to send a servant, but he could not blame her. Rebecca had her work to do. Besides, his return from the clinic had not been easy. He could not expect to be loved without condition by those who had loved him before, as though nothing had changed. He would take love when it came, he thought, and be grateful. He had learned that in the clinic, where all men's eyes were turned away.

Then Engel had come, and he had taken her on and done his best to smile. You may choose your room, he had said, and she had nodded. I'll have one with the sun then, with the sun in the morning, so that I see it when I wake up. My last job, I lived in a cellar like a rat. They thought I didn't need the light, being a servant, how stupid they were. She shook her body, the kind of slow shake a heavy dog might use to wake itself, and laughed. You let me choose my room, she said, and I swear to you I'll never leave.

She spent the first day walking around the house. Morgan could hear her feet on the floorboards, as he waited for her to make up her mind. He heard doors open and close, and words he couldn't catch, as though she were discussing the merits of each room with another person, in a language he felt he recognized but couldn't place. Now and again, she laughed at something, or remonstrated.

The room she chose in the end was on the same floor as his, and had not been intended for a servant. It was large and square, with wallpaper of white and yellow vertical stripes, white flowers on the yellow, yellow flowers on the white, a room that looked southeast towards the distant hills. Next to it was a bathroom, with a deep white tub on four clawed feet and gilded taps with porcelain lozenges that bore the words *chaud* and *froid* in italic script. There was a fireplace in both rooms, and a carpet in the bedroom. When he saw this, Morgan remembered his mother shouting at a girl to be more careful or she would burn the carpet, and the girl crying. He'd sworn then that he would never make a servant cry.

Most of the carpets in the house had been sent back by his grandfather, who had travelled the world before settling in Persia. He had lived there for many years and grown rich and then designed this house, which he never saw, with the help of a French architect he knew there. It was typical of him that he had died on the way home, on the boat, of an infection, despite all his medical pretensions. He had lived in his own country for less than a third of his life and, by his own account, had never been happy until he was finally away, an explorer first, a man of business second. It was fitting that he, who had been obsessed by illness, should have been defeated by something as trivial as an ear infection.

When Engel arrived, Morgan had already spent as many years enclosed in this house as his grandfather had spent in his own country, yet even then he was not sure whether he would call it home. He would call parts of it home perhaps. Yet he was sure that Engel would say from that first day that the room she chose was home to her. When she showed him which one she'd chosen, opening the door in her matter-of-fact way and ushering him in, her few belongings already unpacked and laid out on the bed, he saw at once that the room was full of Engel. There was no other way to say it. Even if the walls had been faded grey and the carpet scorched, the room would be bursting with Engel.

# CHAPTER THREE

in which medical help is required and
Morgan is shocked by an image in water

It was Engel who called for the doctor the first time, when Daisy began to cough. Despite his anxiety, Morgan was reluctant, knowing how little doctors could do, but Engel insisted. You can't just have children and then not care for them, you must see that, she said. It's all very well for you to think that doctors are no use, yet where would you be without them? I would be dead, he said, and let her think about that for a moment. Then, because he could see that she was close to shouting with frustration but also perhaps because his words had been cruel, he relented.

You must find me a doctor who is discreet, he specified. A doctor who can keep his mouth shut, because what we have done here will not be tolerated. There will be someone out there who will make us pay. Engel nodded, then wiped her hands on her apron. Just let them try to take our children away from us, she said, her mouth set. They'll see what happens if they do. How odd, he thought, that she should presume so much, the unexpectedness of this joint parentage taking his breath away for a moment; yet he was, perhaps more than anything else, flattered. Our children, he thought. Sometimes he wanted to touch her, just brush the perfect skin of her forearm with his hand, but he never did. Boundaries protected them both. Besides, he couldn't bear

21

the thought that she might feel, at his touch, disgust rise in her craw and be obliged to hide it from him. It was always a wonder to him when the babies reached up and stroked his face with their tiny feeling hands, a wonder they seemed to share. He watched, his breath caught in his throat, as their pale eyes opened wide, their fingertips with nails no bigger than a grain of rice exploring the ragged seams and creases of his cheek and chin and lip, although he himself felt nothing; there was no pain, at least. Not anymore. He let them hold his own finger in their hands and take it to their mouths. He let them chuckle and dribble and suck. He would let no one deprive him of this.

Engel did what was required with skill and discretion. Morgan never troubled to ask her how or where she had found Doctor Crane. There seemed no point. He knew that it would be all right the instant he saw the Doctor take Daisy in his arms and lift her until their noses were almost touching, and whisper something that made Daisy laugh and turn her head away. Doctor Crane was tall and thin, big-boned, with large white teeth and fairish hair brushed back, though it would not stay back. He was too young to be a doctor, thought Morgan, though this could not have been the case; he was perhaps Morgan's age. But he looked and behaved like someone too young to be serious all the time, as doctors had to be. His trousers were short on him, as though he hadn't finished growing. His wrists stuck out bare and bony from the sleeves of his ill-fitting jacket. He had a large impetuous voice, large and urgent though incapable of harshness, that seemed to have just broken. He blushed when Engel said he was a figure of a man.

Morgan saw the Doctor but the Doctor didn't see

Morgan. Engel had taken the Doctor into the green drawing room off the hall, a small room with symmetrical alcoves designed for statues, two sofas covered in olive-green silk, and a fireplace made of dark pink basalt brought from Egypt. Morgan was concealed in one of the alcoves by a curtain of heavy brocade, into which he had cut a spyhole. He had a view of the centre of the room, between the pair of sofas. Engel made sure Daisy was examined where he could see them, guiding the Doctor to a preestablished point on the carpet, also from Egypt. He watched as the Doctor listened through his stethoscope to Daisy's chest and back and examined her throat, holding her tongue down with what appeared to be (and was, as Engel confirmed later) a silver apostle's spoon. He heard, with relief, the words of the Doctor as he turned to Engel and said, It's nothing of importance, nothing to worry about, a touch of cold, only natural in this frigid weather, and prescribed a cough tincture and a few days' rest. That was when Engel offered him coffee and he rubbed his hands together like a boy, and Morgan knew they'd be safe with him. They left the room and Morgan waited for a moment before coming out from behind the curtain and smiling at Daisy in his own way. She giggled and raised her arms to be lifted. There are children who are only happy when their faces are buried in the neck of adults, Morgan had learned. Daisy was one of these. She gave a little sigh, like a hiccup. He put one arm beneath her bottom and held her to him as he crept across the hall, an intruder in his own home, and let himself into the scullery. From there, through a small glass vent in the wall, he could see into the kitchen. The house lent itself so completely to his need for secrecy it seemed as though his grandfather had foreseen it all, his grandson's disfigurement and withdrawal, his shame for what he was and could not change.

They were sitting together, Engel and Doctor Crane, at the table. They each had a mug of steaming coffee, freshly made, and Engel had cut some slices of fruit cake and put them on the table. She was asking him if he was married. The Doctor's mouth was full of cake, but he shook his head, and she laughed and said he was a proper catch for a woman, he should look out.

David walked into the kitchen and halted; he hadn't expected a visitor. He was old enough to know that visitors were not encouraged at the house; perhaps he was old enough to know why. Sometimes, David would look at Morgan with other, older, eyes and Morgan would think it was only a matter of time before he turned away and looked no more.

Doctor Crane stood up and held out his hand. Morgan was proud to see David take the man's hand and introduce himself. He said that he was David and that he had no mother or father and that it was of no importance because Engel looked after him like a mother. And Daisy is your sister, the Doctor said, not as a question, but as a statement of fact. Morgan still held Daisy in his arms; she wriggled to be put down and he was afraid they would be discovered. But she grew calm again when David said, in his formal way, Yes, Daisy is my sister. I have other sisters and brothers. Perhaps you would like to meet them?

When they left the kitchen, Morgan couldn't follow them any further without being seen. He put Daisy down and together they were walking through the scullery when he heard what sounded like Engel and David approaching. In a panic, he swept Daisy into his arms and carried her out to the garden and down the nearest path, which led to the boathouse by the lake.

It was little more than a large pond, but it had always been called the lake. When he came here as a child, before he had learned to swim and then to row, it had seemed as large as the sea. The boathouse was also modest, a shed that overhung the water, with a rowing boat housed inside. Morgan hadn't been here since the accident three years before. He put his finger to his mouth, so that Daisy would know she had to keep quiet, and opened the door. The boat was covered with a tarpaulin. The stains were still on the floor; no one had cleaned them away. He hurried across, not quite sure why. Perhaps he thought they could hide beneath the tarpaulin and pretend this was a game. But Daisy hung back; she was scared, he could see that, and pale as well. How old was she? Four? She had a cough that could settle in her lungs. What was he thinking of, bringing a sick child to this damp, cold place? Engel would be furious with him when she found out.

He turned and stumbled, landing with his knees on the wooden floor. His head was near the surface of the water, which bobbed inside the boathouse, dark and scented. He struggled to rise, dipping towards the water as he did so, and the face of a monster loomed up towards him, a monster with bared white teeth and an eye that never closed. He cried out, a dreadful gasping cry torn from the bottom of his lungs, and crawled away from the edge of the platform. The monstrous face slid back like a blade beneath a piece of skin and disappeared beneath his knees. Daisy was curled behind him on the floor, her arms round her head, shaking with fear or cold. Struggling to his feet, he scooped her up and hurried towards the house.

This was the second time since the accident that he had seen his own face. The first had been in the clinic, when a nurse had left him alone in one of the bathrooms by mistake. The clinic, which specialized in cases like his, was almost entirely bare of mirrors, but this bathroom had a cabinet above the basin, which was known to contain a mirror the size of a postcard. Sometimes, because they had no choice, the other men would joke about it. They ought to put one of those special mirrors there, that you can see through from behind, and charge people entrance, one of them said. Sixpence for the horror show. What he didn't understand was why, when he had seen their faces, he had supposed that his would be bearable. Despite what his searching fingers had found, dead skin pushed into seams and troughs, and the knowledge of the pain, which did not leave him, he had imagined that he would recognize himself.

The nurse found him on the bathroom floor, weeping, and took him away. No, no, not back to the others, he said. Not like this. Not yet. He felt as though they too would see, for the first time, what he had seen.

Engel was standing at the French window, her hands on her hips. Morgan paused in the middle of the lawn, Daisy's arms tight round his neck, and tried to reassure himself that the Doctor had gone. But Engel stepped outside. Bring her here at once, she cried, in a voice that was new to Morgan. He flinched and did as he was told. Something quite unforeseen had happened and he had been thrown into a state of loss. He felt confused and, more cuttingly, exposed, as if to ridicule. Exposed to his own ridicule, he thought, since no one else had seen what he had seen, and here in front of him was Engel, bundling the child away from him, where she settled with a little sigh, already half asleep; Engel, who saw Morgan every day and didn't seem to see his face at all. Perhaps it was not a face she saw but a mask, behind which he was nonetheless, to her at least, perfectly visible.

# CHAPTER FOUR

in which Morgan's library is
described and Moira speaks

In the first few months after coming home, for want of anything better to do, Morgan had started what he saw as his long and empty life alone by cataloguing the charts and books in the main library downstairs. The charts, of seas and countries, of coasts and mountain ranges, had been made by his grandfather and followed his early travels. They were laid flat in special drawers and had the scent of the places they had been made; aromas of myrrh and ambergris floated through his head as he lifted each chart carefully onto the table to examine it. The charts, of seas and

But most of the room was devoted to books. His grandfather had kept a collection of books, most though not all on medical matters, and had also purchased, through an aide, two gentlemen's libraries at auction, and had them folded into one, which meant that many books on the shelves existed in at least two copies. Morgan began by writing the details of each book on a file card, the kind used in public libraries, and arranging them in deep black trays. He wrote the name of the book and of its author and then, with a wholly unnecessary bibliographic flourish, recorded its date of publication and size. He had found a book on books, so to speak, which helped him to do this, providing the measurements, in inches, of octavo, quarto, duodecimo, and so on. When a card already existed for a book, he would take the volumes and compare them, preferring sometimes the better copy and sometimes the worse. He let his instinct guide him. The preferred copy was taken upstairs to Morgan's book room, which used to be his father's study.

The work absorbed him. He saw the books first as objects that demanded his attention, like insects or lacquered boxes. Many of them dealt with local matters, because the gentlemen who had owned them were local men. There were books about the history of the county and fox hunting, books about the old religion and the Reformation, books that described the houses and lands of the rich, small much-consulted books on estate management. For Morgan, who had no interest in the world outside the borders of his property, these books existed to be classified, not read. There were numerous copies of *Punch* and the *Illustrated London Magazine* and *Blackwood's*, bound into volumes and stamped with the year. Both men had collected these periodicals, and had them bound, though neither copy seemed to have been much read. Morgan also felt no desire to read these works. Sometimes, though, as he wrote out a title on the index card, his tongue between his teeth, he would feel an urge to put down his pen and open the book to see what it contained and find himself reading an article about Dundee or the Seven Wonders of the Ancient World, or wondering if cartoons of the sort he discovered, though finely drawn, had ever made people laugh. Books of travel delayed him as his grandfather's charts had, with their descriptions of places he would never see; books with maps and the names of distant cities. Antioch. Cathay. Jerusalem. Like the scent of spices from the charts that had tickled his palate before. The older books spoke of places with monstrous people, who used their single feet like parasols to protect themselves from the sun, or lived on air and water. These books he would thumb through, pausing to savour paragraphs before continuing with his cataloguing. Works of philosophy and moral thought attracted him, and he would set their cards aside for later, for when he had time to read was how he put it to himself, aware that there was no time other than the present and that he could expect another fifty years of that.

But the book that interrupted him was entitled *A History of Masks*. It had been published over a century ago and was richly illustrated, with hand-coloured drypoint etchings protected by sheets of tissue paper, the line of glue along the inner edge the colour of weak tea. The first illustrations were of Greek theatre, where the role of the masks was merely ritual. Morgan was rapidly bored by these archetypes of tragedy and comedy, lust and derision; they seemed to him to conceal nothing, but simply to be—there was no face behind them, but only the physical form of the bearer, whose task was to move the mask around the stage. Not even the audience cared what lay behind. What sense did a mask have, he wondered, if to remove it meant nothing?

He turned to the next section. Here were Italian masks from Naples and Florence and Venice, dating back to the Renaissance. These were often small; the concealment they offered was a sort of titillation. Morgan was intrigued by these slips of papier-mâché and silk and finely worked animal hide. Here, in these masks of occasion, the final purpose was to be revealed. He imagined galas and carnivals, when people would fall in love as much with what they imagined as with what they saw before them.

Later sections were devoted to the masks of Africa and Asia and North America. Here, Morgan felt that he was searching for something that he knew would not be there, his own new face made out of leather and conch shells. He wanted to see what the mask would look like that had no face beneath it; the mask that had become the face. He wanted to see if anyone had lived with the living face removed and only the mask remaining, pressed and sealed to the bone. But the writer had no interest in the notion that faces and masks might be interchangeable, or that the lines between them might be blurred. Morgan had not occurred to him.

One day, Morgan stopped reading and began to write. He prepared his desk. He found the typewriter his mother had used for letter writing, a black-and-gold cast iron object as tall as it was wide, and arranged for ribbons to be sent, which took some weeks and much anxiety. He had a ream of clean white paper placed beside an empty tray he planned to fill with words. This was around the time he had the windows boarded up and covered with extra shelves. Each morning, after finishing his breakfast, he would come to the book room and put a sheet of paper in the typewriter and wait for words to come. Sometimes they did. They were never the words he wanted, but sometimes they would do. He wrote about the objects he saw in his room to start with, to limber up, minute descriptions of the chair and desk, of the typewriter itself, that caused him immense effort.

He had never *seen* anything before. After a while, when everything that surrounded him had been described, he turned to the subject of masks in a mood of angry frustration and determination. He would say what the book hadn't said. He would say what he knew.

The first few pages he wrote were ponderous and confused. There were too many things a mask could be used to do, and Morgan lost himself in cavils and qualifications. In the end, he closed his eye and pushed the typewriter away.

He started to write again after Engel and the children arrived, but this time he chose not to write about himself. He wrote about his grandfather, the stories he had been told by his mother as a child. There were hundreds of these, phrases and anecdotes and longer, more intricate tales that occupied many pages. Sometimes, he would sit with the end of his pen in his mouth and dream, then set himself back, with a shake, to the task at hand.

Morgan's mother had always said Morgan looked like his grandfather, but was more handsome, and she had shown him photographs to prove it, though he couldn't see the likeness. To Morgan, every face was different, there were no likenesses. Certainly, though, his grandfather had been handsome.

Most photographs of him had been taken abroad. He had seemed to enjoy dressing up in the local fashion, posing in turbans and caftans and decorated robes of various kinds, with pointed shoes and hats and a series of weapons, real and ornamental, that dangled from sashes and belts. He had the air of an adventurer, which was what he was.

These were the things that Morgan wrote. He wrote

about the commercial empire his grandfather had created and maintained between his own country, in which he barely set foot any longer, and the Middle East. He wrote about the year his grandfather had spent in a jail in Cairo, in a cell with a hundred other men, because he had been confused with someone else. He wrote about how his grandfather, upon his release, had begun to study medicine, that of the Arabs, which he referred to as the original medicine, and then the medicine of his own country, filling notebooks with scribbles that were barely legible, collecting specimens from every part of the world, injecting himself with potions and dirt and then more potions, so that he would pass days, and sometimes weeks, in a state of modulated fever. His grandfather had seemed to be searching for something to cure an illness that had still to be defined; he had got everything back to front. And as Morgan wrote, stiff-backed and upright, he forgot about his face for hours on end. Which made it all the worse when he remembered.

Moira would often lie beside him in the finely carved sandalwood cot that had once been his, which Engel pushed from room to room as Morgan ordered. He wanted to watch Moira grow; more important, he wanted her not to lose sight of what he was; familiarity protected them both from shock. When she murmured or cried or gurgled, he turned from the typewriter and stroked the hair from her face, touched when she caught his hand and pulled it to her mouth to be sucked on and dribbled over. She said his name once, he was sure of it, and, shortly after, that of Engel, though Engel wasn't there to hear. She will never say Mummy or Daddy, Morgan thought, but that was just as well. To say Morgan and Engel would be enough; these words were also tokens of love.

But then one day she did say *maman*, quite distinctly, when he lifted her out of the cot, towards his face, because he couldn't resist putting her to the test, to see if she would flinch or touch. She said *maman* to him. He hugged her to his chest, as Engel so often did, enthralled by this mistake. Where did the word come from? he wondered. Who could have taught it to her? Had it been waiting, bubbling under, for its moment? Had she been made in order that this word be uttered? No, he said gently, because it wouldn't have been honest not to correct her, and he would always be honest with his children, with all his children, I'm Morgan. Morgan. He let her finger touch his lip as he spoke so that she could feel the word as well. He knew that he hissed when he had to pronounce certain sounds, the letters *s* or *f*, but he had been fortunate in that; he could still say his name.

# CHAPTER FIVE

*in which Doctor Crane returns to the house*

The second time Doctor Crane came was for Moira, who had been suffering from a high temperature for days. This time, Engel took Crane into the largest of the sitting rooms. Morgan had arranged his seat behind a Chinese screen, a series of hinged, lacquered panels with a row of diamond-shaped holes, at eye level for someone sitting, as Morgan was. Engel had watched him set this up with evident irritation, which he had tried to ignore, successfully at first. This had encouraged her to begin to tut, initially under her breath, the noise gradually increasing in volume as Morgan arranged the screen to his satisfaction and chose the most suitable chair, suitably upholstered because he might be there for some time. Eventually, he had asked her what was wrong, with a waspish tone. Was there something that offended her? Well, she said, nothing, I suppose. You're making an awful lot of noise about nothing, he said. The noise I make is my affair, she said. Lord knows, it isn't my place to tell you what to do. He was silent; he knew that the best way to make Engel talk was to challenge her by silence. In the end, she began, like a blocked pipe that suddenly breaks and pours out water everywhere. It's all the same to me, she said, if you're too proud to let the Doctor see you. Too proud to let a man of science look at your face. A good man, it's shining out of him; he wouldn't hurt a fly if he could help it, his good hands, his good heart, you can see his goodness in every ounce of him. Do you think I don't know a good man when I see him?

It's not a question of pride, he said, but shame. At this, Engel gave a scornful grunt. And what have you to be so ashamed of? You didn't do it to yourself, did you? And isn't he a doctor, for goodness' sake? Don't doctors look at men like you every day of their lives and live with it? What good is a doctor that can't look at a man and see a man? You let me look, don't you? Where's the shame in that? Are you ashamed with me?

Morgan listened to this, his face averted, but did not speak. She was right, of course, he had been seen by doctors a thousand times. He had been examined and pored over and reproved and commiserated with, because they had done all they could and it was not enough, and he was aware, as they spoke among themselves and to him, that all they were asking from him was forgiveness. We know the extent to which we have failed, they seemed to want to say; we know that what you are is hidden beneath what we have made of you, despite our efforts, and that it will never be uncovered because it no longer exists. And yet they were filled with pride as well, and rightly so, because they had brought him back from the brink of death. They had dragged him back to life and given him what was nothing if not a face, though what kind of face it was they wouldn't say. He did feel a sort of gratitude, not for the work they had done but for the fact that they had done it, that they had thought him worth it. He was grateful for that, he couldn't deny it; for the generosity of their intentions. Which was why he had never had the heart to tell them that he would rather have died than live like this. That he would never forgive them for what they had done, for the patchwork of mortified flesh into which their efforts had transformed him. That he would willingly wish his face on them, on each of them, if that meant that he would be free of it, even in death he would wish it on them. He would never forgive them for assuming that he would wish to live, for assuming that all life, of any kind, was to be preferred to death.

Yet what blame did Doctor Crane have in all of this? Engel was right. He was more than a good doctor, he was a good man; that had been clear from the way he treated Daisy. What Engel had meant was that he was worthy of my trust, thought Morgan. He stood there, thinking all this, when the door knocker sounded. Engel came back into the room, wheeling Moira in the carved cot of Indian sandalwood that had once been Morgan's, and with Doctor Crane, in his long grey overcoat, one step behind. They were all three of them in the room before the Doctor noticed Morgan.

"Oh my poor man," he said, walking towards him, his hand held out. "Who has done this to you?" And Morgan shook his head, taking the hand and holding it tightly, with a strange sense of joy, because he had been recognized.

"No one," he said. "It was an accident."

He had sworn to himself, in his ward in the clinic, that he would never do this, yet less than three hours later, when the two men were sitting opposite each other at the kitchen table, he found himself telling the story of the accident as he had never told it. Perhaps if Engel had asked him, he might have opened his heart to her; but she had never asked. He had always thought: She doesn't need to know; she knows. Yet he didn't feel that this was the case with the Doctor.

Morgan needed to tell him; he needed to let the Doctor know that what had happened to him could, after all, be shared. He felt that the Doctor had given his permission for this. This is why the expression *opening his heart* was the right expression to describe what he was doing; because it was a gift both of love and of revelation. He talked, and while he talked the Doctor reached over and held Morgan's two bare hands, the good one and the wounded one, between his. And all the while Engel sat beside them, in her armchair by the fire, with Moira asleep like a cat in her lap. Morgan talked, and this is what he said.

# CHAPTER SIX

in which Morgan explains his injuries to Doctor Crane

I don't want to sound vain and I don't want to seem ridiculous because how can anyone who looks the way I do now say that he was once handsome without making himself seem ridiculous. But it's true. I was extraordinarily handsome when I was young. I was a beautiful child, everyone said so, and I became an even more beautiful boy. I have always hated vanity and now, the way I am, it feels like the greatest deceit of all, like the summoning of evil to my aid; but nothing will otherwise be understood, you see. Beauty is a two-edged sword; it gives and it takes. In my case, it made me hard to love and easy to admire, by my mother at least. She would look at me and see her own beauty reflected, because she too was a famous beauty and I had inherited my features from her; but she would also be challenged by what she saw. I was years younger, and a boy, which gave me a sort of power she would never have. That's what she must have thought. When people came I would be shown off, she used to treat me as an exhibit; I was her beauty's ambassador. She had me dressed in a way that exalted my fine straight limbs and the fine and even features of my face. I still have some photographs of that time; someday, perhaps, I'll show you them. She didn't care to show off my younger sister so much. Rebecca took after my father's side of the family and was pretty in a different way, less pretty I suppose than I

39

was, though pretty isn't the word for what I was, there is no depth to pretty; perhaps this was why my mother loved me more. I think that she only understood what she felt for Rebecca when it was too late, when she had nothing in the house but me and her two wolfhounds.

As I grew taller and my mother weaker, because she suffered from a slow crumbling of the bones that gave her great pain and made all movement difficult, she used me as a sort of crutch, with the wolfhounds bounding around us as her escort, like some pagan goddess. I learned to walk at her pace and pause as she did as we wandered around the garden and she led me down to the lake, where she would examine the water lilies and other plants that grew there, which she had introduced, and then down to the wooded part at the far end of the lawns, beyond the rose beds and the vegetable garden, among the rhododendrons and azaleas, where the air smelt of mould, until she was tired and would need to pause for breath because she had talked herself out. She never stopped talking, as long as she had breath, she always needed to talk. She would tell me about her childhood, the countries she had lived in, the places she had seen. She told me about the first garden she could remember, which was walled and cool, and about the geckos that had lived there, the baby geckos with their beating hearts visible through the skin, the old ones thick and rough, like old men's hands. She told me about the noise the children made when they saw her, like a little princess, and of how they would run beside her car with their dirty hands pressed to its flanks until it went too fast and they were left in a cloud of dust, and of how the streets were filled with one-eyed cats.

She would use me to speak to the gardeners, telling me

what to say to them as they worked, perfectly aware that she could be heard by them as clearly as by me, enjoying the sound of my voice as I repeated what she had said. She loved gardening, in her way. She was an expert, although she left the dirty work to others, almost all the dirty work, right to the very end. She had her passions, which lasted for a while and were replaced; for aquilegias, cycads, scented phlox, finally orchids. Her tastes would swing from the showy to the subtle, unaware of the strange effect this created, the hodgepodge of colours and forms, oblivious of the extra work it made for her gardeners. She had no sense of the large effect, she worked with details. She used to say she was a slave to her garden, which was nonsense; she was a slave to nothing except her appetites and her needs, which were one and the same. Her greatest need of all, though, was for me, to have me with her, beside her, always. She treated me as something infinitely precious, yet also as she might have treated a household pet, one of her wolfhounds; a creature with no will of its own and no rights; she couldn't see the difference. She made me work for her as a trained animal might have done, some cunning monkey, a source of traction. Sometimes I would row her slowly around the lake until she grew bored; on these occasions she would tell me about her father, her tone a mixture of pride and contempt. She had inherited her grandmother's capacity for scorn.

I didn't go away to school; people had come to me for a few years, and so I had learned to read and write, some simple arithmetic, a sprinkling of languages; various tutors, young men usually, who would fall under my mother's spell and be dismissed as soon as this became obvious. My father would have liked me to go away to school, I think;

my grandfather, I know, would have insisted, simply to free me from the stifling company of women. But this was all my mother's doing; I was her only business, in the end. She had lost her first child, my brother, Ralph, two years before I was born, when a typhoid epidemic killed a dozen boys and two masters at his school. He died without her, she never forgave him that. That's how selfish she was. After his death, she saw schools as unhealthy, disease-ridden places of death. Besides, my father invariably let her do what she wanted; he was scared of her anger, which she doled out in small hard doses for days and even weeks until he had forgotten its cause. He would confide in me, yet even with me he seemed wary. He said to me more than once that to see my mother and me together was to be breathless with pride. I think he had always been afraid of her, and so he was of me as well. I think he also loved my sister more than he loved me, perhaps because she was simpler to love. He would have given her the factory in any case, I think. I would have liked to have spent more time with him, to learn how to be a man, but he was almost never at home; he was almost a stranger to me. He worked abroad for many years, in my grandfather's company, buying and selling, I'm not sure what. Spices were part of it, but also, I think, weapons. Perhaps weapons more than anything. I wonder sometimes if that is what the factory is making. I would have liked to study him, and to have him study me, to see what I might become.

I didn't know many other boys, three or four sons of family friends, with whom I would sometimes be sent to play while the adults stayed in the house and talked among themselves. I saw these boys as enviable. I didn't feel safe with them, and I liked that; I liked the sense of danger they gave me, though all we did was play the kind of games boys always play, dividing ourselves between the forces of good and bad, like kittens learning to hunt, first one on top and then the other. Afterwards, when they had gone, my mother would ask me if I had enjoyed myself and what she wanted was for me to say no, that I preferred to stay with her. I didn't say this, although I may have let her think it. My sister was sent away to school, you see, as soon as she was old enough, when she was six; my mother said that girls were tougher than boys and could fight off disease; I was the child to be kept at home; that was my privilege and my punishment. After a while, the other boys stopped coming, around the time the last of my tutors was also dismissed, I must have been thirteen or fourteen. Perhaps it was fear that stopped them, because of what was happening outside, but I think now that their parents were no longer invited because my mother had begun to be ashamed of her body, which was crippled by illness. Her back bent sideways, she had to strain to raise her head. She began to spend her days in bed with her dogs stretched out on the floor beside her like enormous rugs. I would read to her. The books she liked best were stories of the rich. Her favourites were biographies of women aristocrats who had lived in France before the revolution, and been condemned and had gone bravely or unknowingly to their death. Hah, she would say as I read aloud the description of the final ride in the tumbrel to the guillotine, with an exhalation of bitter satisfaction, as though she had been proved right after all. The first signs of her madness were these, I think, the delight she took in hearing of the violent deaths of women she admired and emulated.

Because she saw herself as aristocratic to her bones, she'd grown to feel that the circumstances of my grandfather's birth had cheated her of her natural rank. She never forgave her mother for marrying beneath her. My father used to sit beside her on the bed when I was there and hold her hand, which was beginning to lose its beauty, but he didn't speak because there was nothing to be said, by him at least. I know now that he had no idea of what she wanted, of how he might have tempered her suffering; he had no idea that her suffering was entirely self-inflicted. He thought I knew, but he was wrong. He treated me like a priest or shaman, and I didn't know how to tell him she was also a mystery to me, her rage, her selfishness. It's only now that I begin to understand her, perhaps at this very moment, as I am talking to you. Sometimes she would take my face in her hands, and stare into my eyes with her mad eyes, as if she was using me as a mirror, the only mirror that would show her what she needed to see, and even that only intermittently. She'd turn my face here and there as if to seek it. And then she would cast it away, and sigh with frustration.

The first time she hurt herself was with a knife she kept from the lunch tray, before it was taken back to the kitchen. I found her sawing at her forearm with it. When I walked in, she threw the knife down in a fury. This is no good, she cried, it won't cut. It won't cut *properly*. She held out her arm to show me like an angry child. I saw a dozen welts in rough parallel, but no broken skin. The knife was a fish knife, we had eaten smoked haddock poached in milk that day, and I still remember a smear of yellow where she had made the first attempt to cut her arm, after which the knife was clean. She had a sulky, peeved expression on her face, as though a toy had broken. I didn't know what to do, so I took the knife from her gently, washed it in the bathroom basin, and told no one. Later, I put it back in the kitchen drawer and thought, well, that's the end of it. I was fifteen.

Three or four months passed before she did anything else like that. I had taken her into the garden, pushing her chair along the path to the rose garden. She was laughing, I remember, because the dogs were behaving like puppies, kicking their legs in the air and barking, and I felt almost proud of her, because she seemed so brave. By then she was in constant pain. She was talking about her plans for the garden, about what she would do that autumn; a large new herbaceous border filled with acid-lovers, the big wisteria on the boathouse pruned. At times what she said made no sense at all, at other times she was perfectly lucid and often amusing, particularly when she talked about my father and what a sweet and useless man he was; she knew full well what she was saying then.

I pushed her until she could reach out and touch the rosebushes. Closer, closer, she insisted, drumming her fingers impatiently on the armrests of the chair. I want to smell them. There was one in particular she loved, with large veined pink-and-white flowers, I don't remember the name, although she must have said it a hundred times in my presence. It was one of the oldest bushes, a tangle of massive knotted stems and thorns and as soon as she was close enough she pulled one of the thicker stems with a burst of strength that astonished me and dragged the thorns across her face. She's trying to blind herself, I thought, and I was right. I pulled the chair back and she flung herself forward somehow into the roses, her body a live weight in the middle of the bush. Mother, I cried, Mother, but she was twisting and writhing into its heart, making a low moaning noise, I heard her say *yes yes yes*, and I grabbed her by the back of her dress, by the skirt of it, and started to drag her out. The thorns had hooked themselves to the material, I heard a ripping. She was light enough by then, it was her rage that made her heavy; as soon as I had pulled her up, I grasped her round the waist, I had never held her that close before, she wriggled like a child. I couldn't see her face. She struggled and writhed, scratching the backs of my hands with her broken nails and crying *put me down damn you put me down you have no right,* while spots of blood splashed down on my sleeve. When she was back in the chair, her body hunched with malevolence and fury, I saw how much damage she had done. Her face was covered with scratches, some of them deep, each of them bleeding—most of her cheeks and chin and forehead were smeared deep red; rose petals were stuck to the blood. One of her eyes was blinking closed and she was moaning. At first I thought she was moaning with pain, but I was wrong; she was moaning with frustration. Finally she came back to herself. *Well don't just stand there you little fool*, she cried. *I'm your fault now.*

She had scratched the cornea of her left eye, and the scratch became infected. The local doctor wasn't up to it, he always seemed to be one step behind the problem. Perhaps you knew him? I don't remember his name. By the time he decided that she needed to be examined by a specialist, when the eyelids were nothing but a pus-closed fissure, it was too late; the sight in that eye was gone. She never complained; in that way she was admirable. The other result was that my father began to say she should be placed somewhere

else, where she could be helped more effectively. That was
the word he used, *placed*, like an ornament he'd acquired
somewhere and brought home. Although back in the country
now, he was still away much of the time, from Monday to
Friday and often at weekends. He was in charge of what
was left of my grandfather's business, so he only knew about
the big events, not the day-to-day strangeness of her. He
really had no idea what was happening. He didn't want her
to be helped particularly, I don't think; generally, people
who say this don't. What he wanted was for the problem of
her to be solved. He wanted her out of his life because he
didn't know how to cope with her, she was too big for him,
although all he ever saw were the edges of her, the thorns
and spikes and husk of her. I was the one who lived *within*
the world of her. I was the one who washed her dozen tiny
wounds, made with her fingernails if nothing else was to
hand, and fed her and heard her say *fuck* a hundred times
in succession and then laugh and say that no one had ever
loved her, no one, and that this was how she had wanted it,
she hadn't needed love, not even from me; these last words
spat at me like poison spray. I let her do all this, how could
I have prevented it? I didn't know what the right thing to
do was, there was no one there to ask, no one I trusted; I
let her do whatever came into her head. I mentioned my
sister to her once, I don't remember in what connection,
because she was almost never at home, perhaps I had said
that I missed her, as I often did; and my mother said that she
knew damn well what I wanted *her* for, the slut, for my filthy
jiggery-pokery, because I was filthy, like all men, I would
fuck her blind. I wasn't surprised, it was the kind of thing
my mother often said, but I wondered if it was true that I

was like all men, because that would mean that I *was* a man, or sufficiently like one to be the thing itself. I had no sense of other men, no way to measure what might be the man in me. My father had never been the sort to encourage me, as the fathers of other boys seemed to do; as my grandfather would have done, I think, though I never knew him. My father had left me to my mother, as though he wouldn't in any case have known what to do with me. I was yet another of her mysteries.

Then that came to an end as well, when he died in a traffic accident on the way back from town one Friday evening, and I knew that I was the man after all, I had no other choice; I was the man of the house, as the lawyer told me in his vacuous way, although my mother would still have control of the estate for another eighteen months, until I had come of age. She behaved herself with great dignity that day, when the will was read; no one seemed to think it strange that a madwoman should be left to hold the reins of a great fortune. Perhaps I should have said something. But I was nineteen and a half and convinced of my abilities; besides, I was sure my mother had become too crippled to do herself or anyone else serious damage. Her words of anger had come true. Despite what the lawyer had said, she was my responsibility.

In one sense, of course, she was utterly in control, though it wasn't clear to me then. I had the run—and the running— of the household, my mother opposed me in nothing; my father's business I left in the hands of my father's deputy, who managed everything, to the best of my knowledge, with perfect competence until my sister took over. I have never had money problems, which also marks me out, I suppose. On my twentieth birthday I had no notion of any life outside the walls of this house, the walls of this garden; within these inner and outer walls, I thought, I had perfect knowledge. Yet I had no idea that my mother was also possessed of knowledge, as perfect in its way as mine. She had acquired an electric wheelchair and moved her bedroom down to the ground floor, a room that opened onto the garden; a ramp was installed and the French window fitted with handles her fingers could manage. This freedom put her in high spirits. She would drive herself around the garden with the wolfhounds running one on each side of the chair, their great tongues hanging out; a twisted woman in bright clothes with an eye patch and two dogs as tall as the back of the chair. After my father's death, she had become more generous to herself, it seemed to me, less keen to do herself harm.

That was when she took up orchids, corresponding with other growers throughout the world. She'd wait for the morning post with fervour. A greenhouse and potting shed had been built for the new plants, near the boathouse; she would spend whole days there. Often, walking from one room to the next, I would hear the buzz of the motor that drove her chair and, crossing to the window, would see her bouncing along a path to some distant corner of the garden with the dogs. New paths of carefully cut and sectioned stone were being laid all the time, to reduce the chance of her being thrown from the chair. She watched while the stones were laid, waving her otherwise useless stick at the workmen, telling them vulgar and complicated jokes; I think they dreaded her.

One of them, a boy called Norman, she would tease until his neck was crimson. Sometimes, I would go to the garden to find her and she would be with this Norman, instructing him in some gardening task, and they would both pretend not to have seen me until I coughed or spoke or shuffled my feet; at which point they would look up at me as though I had intruded. Norman is a good boy, she would say, the implication being that I wasn't; Norman does what I tell him. Briefly, I entertained the idea that she was using him to satisfy her sexual needs, because surely a woman like my mother would have had no qualms about doing that. But I didn't really think so. What I think now is that she may have flattered him in that way, though he didn't deserve it; he was short, round-shouldered though strong, with a pasty skin and a lolling fat bottom lip. She may have used words to arouse him, the filthy words she used with me, and enjoyed his discomfort. In which case, her sexual needs were being met in the way that suited her best. She had always been excited by the humiliation of others.

She liked scaring people too. That was one of the reasons she loved her dogs, for the effect they had on others. She scared me many times as a child. She used to hold my wrist too tightly when she cut my nails. Once she twisted her fingers around it in a sort of bracelet, as hard and fast as she could, until I yelped with pain. That's what children call a Chinese burn, she said. It's only fair you should know. I was making a face once, the way children do, and she said, Be careful, Morgan, one day the wind will change and you'll be stuck like that forever and no one will love you. And she made the same face at me, but worse because she was an adult, until I began to cry and begged her to stop. This was before the other signs of her illness had become apparent. Perhaps she wasn't ill at all in the end, but simply more revealed.

Norman must have helped her get hold of what she needed, though he always denied it, to the police, to everyone; it wouldn't have been that difficult in any case, not with orchids in the greenhouse. Who knows what she gave him to make him do what she wanted? Perhaps she simply withdrew her disapproval. Perhaps she was simply nice to him. Whatever she did, he helped her prepare what she must have known to be her final act.

The knowledge my mother possessed was that she would sooner be dead than alive; this was sustained by her courage and certitude, which may both in themselves be forms of madness. I thought I would always know what to do with her, what steps to take to prevent her from harm, self-inflicted or otherwise, and I was utterly wrong. Yet even she hadn't known everything, as it turned out.

The last day, we couldn't find her anywhere. We searched in the house, the ground floor first and then, knowing this was foolish, the other floors of the house. Outside, it had been raining heavily for thirty, maybe forty hours, the garden was grey and sodden and smelt of the earth. Nobody thought she would have gone out in it, she hated bad weather. I called the dogs' names, in vain, which worried me more than anything. Then it occurred to me that Norman might know where she was. I had the head gardener sent to my study. I watched a girl run down the path to his house with a large black golfing umbrella, then return moments later with herself and the man beneath it, a dripping canopy with four swift feet. The man stood at the door, I beckoned him in. I'm looking for my mother, I said. I thought Norman might know where she was. I waited. I said, Perhaps you can tell me where Norman is. The man looked ashamed, he shook his head. I wouldn't rightly know, he said, I think he's in the boathouse. By rights, that's where he is. Then why do you say you wouldn't know? I asked him, and he gave a helpless shrug, almost as though I had no right to ask these questions. What on earth's he doing in the boathouse? I said. I expect he'll be working on the boats, the man said painfully, moving his wet boots on the tiles. That's when I knew that he was lying and that I was surrounded by liars, that my mother had been scheming for who knows how long and I had had no idea, she had played me, letting me feel that I was the master. As of course I was. I was always referred to as Master. Master Morgan, the child of the house.

I took the umbrella from the girl and hurried down through the rain to the boathouse. The head gardener was following me, even without the plaintive cries he was making that I should wait, I shouldn't go alone, but I waved him away without turning round, I didn't want witnesses, I didn't want or need assistants; I wanted to be entirely in charge.

The door to the boathouse was closed but not locked. I pushed it open and saw my mother's back crouched over a bench at the far end. The dogs were lying on the floor beside her. There was no sign of Norman. She must have heard me come in, but she didn't turn round or acknowledge my presence; even when I whispered *Mother*. I don't know why I whispered, perhaps because I thought she might be asleep, or dead, and I didn't want to wake the dead. She didn't turn or speak, but I saw her shoulders move slightly, as though she were adjusting her clothes, so I knew she was alive. The rain was beating on the roof, the part of the lake that lay within the boathouse was still and smooth and dark where the rain didn't strike it, puckered and speckled with light where it did. There was an odd smell in the boathouse, sickly sweet but with something pungent underneath. If I had only recognized it, I thought much later, when I was ready for thoughts of this kind; yet how could I have recognized it? I'd never smelt so much blood before. I walked across to her, my wet shoes slipping on the wood, and I had the sensation that when I touched her shoulder she would simply dissolve and I would be left with a handful of empty clothes and this cloying smell, which grew stronger and stronger as I approached. And then I *did* see Norman, behind her, crouched in the shadows and shaking his head as he stared at me, too afraid to speak. He murmured, not looking at me now but at her, *please ma'am*, not once but twice, three times, until the second word no longer sounded like *ma'am* but seemed to be *mum* and I thought, with a jolt of relief, *yes, you're her child*. That was when I saw that both the dogs were dead, their throats slashed open, and I knew that the stink in the place was their blood. I felt it pull on the soles of my shoes as I walked across it and she turned round finally, so that what she had in her hand became visible, yet made no sense, because what I had expected was not a glass jar but a knife. *You can't stop me*, she said and she lifted the jar towards her lips and I remember thinking, before I reached out to stop her, that it was a pickles jar without the lid and I wondered what it had held, as though the mind would do anything rather than know. And then she had thrown it into my face and I began to scream, because I had never imagined such pain. I heard my scream as distant, the work of someone else's throat. I don't know what my mother felt those last few moments, when she had finally freed herself from us all. Norman must have guided me towards the water, where the first bright wave of pain was put out, then dragged me out when I had fainted. By which time she had drunk the rest and was as good as dead.

There is that famous painting, Doctor Crane, of the death of Sardanapalus. Perhaps you've seen it? The dying king is lying on a bed with his wealth around him, the jewels and the jugs and the bowls, his wonderful horses already dead, his concubines being slaughtered by slaves, who will also be killed in their turn. He lounges with one arm supporting his head, surrounded by the carnage his imminent death has triggered, and it is a quiet picture despite its subject, because Sardanapalus is quiet, apparently detached from the scene, soothed to see the destruction of everything he has owned before he also dies, believing that he will find it all around him when he wakes again on the other side of his death, the fragments of porcelain miraculously reunited, the wounds of the women and horses and slaves miraculously healed. I think my mother may have felt like that, in the end. I think her eye was calm as she flung the acid into my face and onto the one hand that flew up to protect it, because the other was clutching at her sleeve, so that now I have one ruined hand and one ruined eye. I think she knew what she was doing and yet felt no responsibility for it, it was her due. And I think she was happy in the end, before she drank what was left in the jar, with her usual greed, because she could never have enough.

# CHAPTER SEVEN

in which Morgan and Doctor Crane decide to play backgammon

Morgan stopped and lowered his good eye from those of the Doctor. He looked down at their hands, together, on the table, and then looked up again, and smiled and the Doctor understood it as a smile, and returned it. And that, said Morgan, is what happened.

Only Engel had noticed David come into the kitchen and listen to every word, from the point at which Morgan had said that he was beautiful. David sat with his eyes wide open and his mouth tight shut. He took Engel's hand in both of his small hands; it rested like a sleeping puppy while his fingers played with it. Then, when Morgan had finished speaking, Engel gently took her hand away and the two men turned from each other's eyes to see the child. David walked to Morgan and climbed into his lap. As soon as he was seated, he looked at Doctor Crane, or at least that was Morgan's impression; all he could see was the back of the small boy's head and, beyond it, the face of the Doctor. When the Doctor smiled and nodded, he understood that David must have spoken in some way and been understood, although he had heard not a single word.

"I shall come on Friday, after lunch," Doctor Crane said in a cautious but determined voice, as though he would not be discouraged. He had made up his mind. "Each Friday afternoon, after lunch, for an hour or two, if I may. You do play backgammon, I hope?"

Morgan nodded. He had no feeling, other than the tremulous vacancy that follows fever. "Yes," he said slowly, unsure of his voice after so much talking. "My mother taught me. She played very well, as ruthlessly as you might imagine. We have a very fine set, from Syria, I believe, with pieces carved from ivory and teak. It will be my pleasure to show it to you."

Crane stood up in his loose ungainly way and smiled, a broad delighted grin that startled Morgan, then looked at Engel. "Perhaps a place might also be laid for me at the dinner table?" he said, almost shyly. "I mean, naturally, on Fridays, after we have played and I have been soundly beaten?" Engel glanced at Morgan, who nodded a second time and smiled and then stood up, lifting David gently to the floor and holding out his good hand to the Doctor.

"Until Friday, then. I shall look forward to it." David ran to the door, to open it and show the Doctor out, and Morgan felt once again that some kind of speech had passed between them, the boy and this sunlike man that Morgan thought of as young, who was, or appeared to be, more or less his own age.

As soon as they were alone in the kitchen, Engel, to his astonishment, pulled him into her bosom. He found himself wanting to laugh as she rocked him, humming a tune he had never heard before yet seemed to recognize, as though all children were born with the knowledge of it.

# CHAPTER EIGHT

in which Doctor Crane describes the world beyond the walls

Doctor Crane was right about being soundly beaten. Morgan turned out to be an imaginative and ruthless backgammon player. He used his good hand to spin the dice onto the board, moving the pieces with a speed that startled and impressed Doctor Crane, for whom the game had never been more than an idle pastime, no more demanding than ludo. When Morgan told him he had played as a child with his mother for entire afternoons, the Doctor was less surprised. After four or five games had been won by Morgan, they would put the board away and talk, or the Doctor would talk and Morgan would listen. Morgan discovered that he was curious once again about the outside world and that Crane could help him satisfy this curiosity. And so they began to talk about the wall.

The wall had been built around the estate when Morgan was still a child, at the start of the troubles. He remembered being taken to see it as it rose above his head, and then above the head of his father, and then far, far above, a wall of dark unglazed brick as thick as an arm was long, with a triangular white stone coping and a row of black iron spikes, like arrowheads. They weren't the only people to take these precautions; other local families constructed similar walls around their properties, while some simply sold up and left the country in planes sequestered by the army and made available to those who could afford one, taking with them whatever was portable of their wealth, leaving the rest behind to be looted and destroyed.

One of Morgan's first memories after the building of the wall was hearing gunfire and shouting and seeing flames rise from beyond it, while he stood with his hand in his mother's and listened to her sing a song he had never heard before, in a language he didn't know. A rebel song, she told him, her dark eyes burning with anger and affront. He didn't know what *rebel* meant. When he found out the meaning, he wondered if he had heard her right. Weren't rebels the ones on the outside, he wondered, the ones who shouted and used their guns and murdered; the ones with a grievance. Perhaps what she had wanted to say was *revel*. She was never happier in those days than when she was preparing for a party of some kind.

Then, without reason as far as Morgan could see, the situation seemed to calm. His father took them to the city and they sat in cafés open to the street and watched the people, just as they might have done before. They didn't seem to be frightened at all as they went about their business, although sometimes children would beg and his mother would give Morgan coppers to reward them with; he would press the coins into their dirty hands with a mingled feeling of distaste and pity, but also a trace of envy as they ran off and giggled together, then turned back to stare at him with a contempt he didn't, at that time, understand. There was terrible poverty, even he could see that. Old people were left outside houses to die; that was how it looked to him; sat up on hard chairs on the pavement and left there for hours on end, then carried back into dark rooms, cellars, and halls, until the next day.

Then his father stopped taking them out because, he told them one evening while they were eating, it was no longer safe to leave the estate, and he loved them all too much to put their lives at risk. Soon after that, he began to travel with a chauffeur, a new man, tall and blond, who spoke a Nordic language and had a gun; the two of them sitting like ghosts behind reinforced glass in his father's powerful blue car, the car that had been towed home after his father's death and still stood, covered in green tarpaulin, in one of the garages behind the house, rusting and immense, a home to generations of nesting rats. From the windows at the top of the house Morgan would watch them enter through the main gate, which was guarded by men who were armed and dressed like soldiers, although his father explained that they were not real soldiers but hired men, because hired men were safer. The army could no longer be trusted. There were tales of what the army did to people, tales that were told in the kitchen and beneath the stairs.

And throughout all this, his mother had gardened. And cultivated orchids.

Now, when Crane began to talk about the world outside, Morgan found himself thinking of the stories he had heard in the kitchen all those years before. He hadn't believed them then and now these new stories seemed equally unlikely. The truth was that, after he had left the clinic and come home, he rarely thought about the world beyond the estate and certainly never regarded it as a threat. The gates had been standing open for months now, because the man who had opened and closed them and kept their hinges oiled was simply not there one morning and had not been replaced. There was no need. Nobody came to the house, or left it.

It had a reputation, Morgan was sure of that. Whenever a new kitchen maid was required, one of the staff would persuade a younger sister or cousin to work for the monster they were never allowed to see, but knew might be lurking; the thought of it kept them obedient. Besides, he paid more than anyone else, thanks to Engel, who arranged their hours and his, to make sure they would never overlap. Engel was no fool.

The Doctor told Morgan that his father and mother had also been doctors. Against the wishes of his father, Crane had trained to be a surgeon. His father had said that the only true doctor was the family doctor, that all the rest were mechanics who dealt with body parts. How can you treat a person, he used to say, when you don't know what his home is like, or the quality of his mother's cooking. A man is a whole thing or he is nothing. For his father, what made a doctor a doctor was his ability to listen. Let them talk, he said, and they will tell you everything you need to know. If what they say is the seed, then you must learn to be the earth. He was right, said Crane, I realized that the first time I cut into a man whose name I didn't know. And so I came back to work with them. And then they died, my mother first and then my father, and I stayed here because the practice would have closed and no one else wanted it. And here I am. He paused and smiled to himself. My father used to like to say: None of my patients is ill but thinking makes him so, is that Shakespeare? Morgan nodded. *Hamlet*, he said. More or less. To me it is a prison.

# CHAPTER NINE

in which Trilby and Pate arrive at the house unannounced

The Doctor and Morgan were playing backgammon in the book room one day when Engel rushed in, flustered, gasping for breath after climbing the stairs. She stood at the door, her large hand on the round brass knob. "They're here," she panted. "They're here for the children. The Lord damn their eyes and ears. They say they're from the government." Both men ran from the room and crossed to the landing window, from which they could see a small grey car parked in the drive. Two men stood beside it, staring up at the rows of dark uncurtained windows. They were dressed identically in black suits, white shirts, black ties, and brown suede shoes. One man was bald, the other wore a narrow-brimmed trilby. Both men were smoking in the same way, with their hands cupped round the end of the cigarette as if to protect the flame, in unison flicking the ash onto the gravel. If they hadn't been smoking, they would have looked like civil servants or plainclothes police. Morgan realized as he watched them examining the house and dropping their ash on his drive that he was trembling, and not for fear of his face being seen, although that was also there, that fear was constant, but because these unwanted, uninvited men might take away their children.

"You have to help me," he said, clutching the Doctor's sleeve.

"Of course," said the Doctor. He turned to Engel. "What exactly did they say to you? What were their words?" His tone was stern. Engel cast her eyes to the ceiling.

"I don't exactly know. I heard them say children, something about our children, and my stomach opened with fright. I thought I would lose my self-respect on the floor in front of them, right there on the floor of the hall. I said I would fetch you at once." She looked at Morgan, hotly ashamed. "I'm sorry, I know I should never have said that. I wasn't thinking. I was *so* scared."

"That isn't important now," said Doctor Crane. He squeezed Morgan's arm. "I'll talk to them." Morgan nodded, then said to Engel, "Take them to the green drawing room. But give me enough time to get behind the curtain." He ran down the stairs, pausing only to assure himself that the front door was properly closed and that he would not be observed. As soon as he was safe behind the curtain, he forced himself to breathe more shallowly. A moment later, Engel opened the door and ushered in the two men, followed by Doctor Crane. Pate took the lead.

"Are you the owner of this house?" he said.

"I am the owner's doctor," Crane said.

Trilby had taken a soft black notebook from his inside breast pocket. He uncapped his pen. "Doctor—?"

"Crane."

"And the owner of the house? Mr.—?"

"Is away at the moment. On business. Perhaps I can help?"

Pate looked suspicious.

"And might I ask what you're doing here in the house

alone, with the owner away? In his house?"

"I would be grateful if you could explain to me first exactly who you are," said Doctor Crane. "And what your business is. Before I answer any more of your questions."

"We're from the ministry," said Trilby.

"The ministry?"

"Of welfare. The ministry of welfare."

"So there is still a ministry of welfare?" said Doctor Crane, with a sniff. "I assumed they'd closed it years ago. For all the welfare I see around me. And you have documents to prove this?"

Both men produced from their jacket pockets a metal plate with their photographs and the symbol of a ministry, a portcullis between two towers. Crane took his time examining these, then gave them back.

"And whose welfare is it exactly that brings you here?" said Crane.

Pate thought about this for a moment, then shook his head as if to dislodge a fly.

"As I said, we'd like to speak to the owner of the house."

"Who is away," said Crane. "As I said."

"It's about certain, well, disturbing rumours that have reached the ministry's ears," continued Pate. "Regarding children."

Morgan's breath caught in his windpipe; for a moment he thought he was going to choke.

"Children?" Crane said.

"We believe there are children here. In the house. Strays."

"Children in the house? In this house? Really?" said Crane, in a tone of ascending surprise. "Might I ask on what grounds you believe this?"

"We have our sources," said Pate in a self-important way, glancing at Trilby, who stood beside him, his pen poised over his notebook. "The ministry, that is to say, has its sources. Which naturally must remain confidential."

"You said *stray* children," Doctor Crane said, slowly, as though the word were new to him. "I'm not sure I quite understand what you mean. In what way might children be considered *stray*?"

Pate looked embarrassed. "It's a ministry term," he said. But Crane insisted.

"Clearly. Which means?"

Pate looked at Trilby, who indicated what appeared to be his permission with a nod; Pate then said, "Well, otherwise unaccounted for, unparented. What used to be termed *orphans*, you might say."

"Unwanted, in other words?"

"That's neither here nor there from the ministry's point of view," said Pate. "Nor from ours, come to that, as ministry servants. It isn't our job to justify the official terminology. These children must be accounted for, that's all. There are *structures*."

"And these *stray* children?"

"Are taken care of by the ministry," said Pate. "Of welfare."

"I understand," said Crane. He glanced for a fraction of a second towards the curtain, one eyebrow raised. It might have been a tic. "In *structures*."

Pate spoke again, with increasing impatience. "Perhaps you would be so good as to answer our questions, Doctor—"

"Crane," said Trilby, reading from his notebook.

"I really don't know what else to say," Crane said. "As

you can see for yourselves," he gestured around him, "there are no children here, *stray* or otherwise. The owner of this fine old house leads a secluded existence, as I'm sure your sources at the ministry will have informed you. He is a man of great culture, a scholar, and appreciates his own company more than any other's. The last thing he would want is the presence of children. When he travels, he does so to ensure himself that his affairs abroad are in order and to experience other civilizations, other worlds. He would hardly want to leave a houseful of children to their own devices. And if you wish to know why I am here, though of what concern my presence might be to the ministry I fail to understand, then I can tell you that the owner of this house is a friend of mine, a dear old friend, whose door is open to me with or without his presence. I am here today, as it happens, to study in the library, which has an extensive collection of medical texts from the last century. I am here to enrich my knowledge. I am certainly not here to gather children, *strays* or otherwise."

Pate said, "We have a warrant."

Crane gestured towards the door. "Indeed? In that case, I'm sure the owner would have no desire to impede you in your ministerial duties. In his absence, I shall be delighted to show you round." He opened the door and waved them both through, not looking towards the curtain. "Perhaps the main rooms on the ground floor first? The house, as you will have realized, is rather large."

As he watched them leave the drawing room, Morgan's heart began to thump against his ribs. His reason told him that his fear was quite unnecessary. Engel, by this time, would certainly have spirited the children away. But perhaps a teddy bear or building brick would have been forgotten, or the small soft shoe of a toddler. Perhaps a cry would escape from the mouth of one of the babies, wherever they were hidden, and be heard by one of these men, these grey-suited jackals with their talk of strays. For one exhilarating second, Morgan entertained the notion that he could spring out from a corner, utter a ghoulish moan, and frighten the men to death; yes, even to death. He could stalk them as they trespassed around his grandfather's house, because it was clear to him that they were trespassing despite their warrant, until the appropriate moment arrived and the horror of his face would do its work. But that would solve nothing, he knew. Then it occurred to him that he could do what he had done the first time the Doctor came; he could hide in the scullery and watch them as they came into the kitchen. Surely they would never search the scullery, he thought. They were from the ministry; the scullery would be beneath them. He lifted the curtain and was about to step into the room when he heard the engine of a car start up and wheels on gravel. Moments later, Crane burst into the room. He couldn't speak for laughter.

"They are *such* fools, *such* idiots," he said finally. "I took them into one of the rooms downstairs and they just stood in the middle of it and looked around as though they'd completely forgotten why they were there. They hadn't got the faintest idea, you know, of what to look for nor how to look for it. They wouldn't have recognized a child, let alone a stray one—you heard that, didn't you? a *stray* child, isn't that the worst of all?—if one had leapt out at them. Mind you," he said, and paused, "they certainly do seem to have disappeared, don't they? The children, I mean. What's Engel done to them?"

"Will they be back, do you think?"

"Heaven only knows." The Doctor was silent. He cocked his head to one side, and Morgan did the same. Not only the Doctor, but the entire house was silent, as though there were no other living being within it than these two men. "Where are they, do you suppose? The children, I mean. Engel must have whisked them away."

Then Morgan said what he had wanted to say to someone, because it had been troubling him, for months now, maybe longer. "Have you noticed," he said, hearing his voice hiss on the final syllable and recalling, as he always did, what thing he was, and realizing, with a start, that to remember implies forgetfulness, and that he had had that moment of forgetfulness and should be grateful, these thoughts so fast they barely registered as thoughts. "Have you ever noticed," he said, "that the children seem to know when they're not wanted, not in the ministerial sense, of course, but, you know, when somebody simply wants to be quiet, I suppose I mean when *I* want to be quiet? They just disappear, they make themselves scarce, as though they've never been in the house at all, as though they've never existed. And then, just when you notice and start to wonder where they are, when you start to worry about them, I suppose, although you might not realize it's worry, it registers as a sort of apprehension, they reappear as miraculously as they disappeared. They pop up from behind a sofa or you hear them crying or calling things out in the garden. But haven't you ever wondered just where they go?" He paused for a moment. When he continued his voice was hesitant. "It's as though they came from the air," he said. And then he told Crane about the arrival of Melissa, expecting to be believed. As he was.

"And hasn't Engel said anything?" the Doctor asked.

"No," said Morgan slowly. "Because that's the other thing. I know it sounds absurd, I hardly like to admit it, but sometimes I have the strong impression that Engel disappears along with them. Sometimes I feel that I'm utterly alone, not just in the house but altogether, in the world in a way, as though none of them had ever been." He was silent for a moment. "I'm not complaining, you must understand. I'm almost happy to feel so alone. If nothing else, it gives me a feeling of security." He paused a second time before adding shyly: "You're the only one who seems real then."

# CHAPTER TEN

in which Doctor Crane and Engel
discuss the nature of disappearance

After this conversation the Doctor seemed to watch the children in a different way. He spent more time than ever before in the house; he wandered the corridors alone, opening the doors to rooms in which the children might be hiding, rooms in which he had seen them play together in the past, only to find them empty. Yet the emptiness seemed recent, as though another, invisible door had only just closed, behind which the children were gathered, holding their breath perhaps so as not to laugh, playing what to them must have seemed a delightful game; and was, except that he had no idea what such a game might mean, other than that he and Morgan were somehow peripheral to it, if not explicitly excluded. Once, he told Morgan, he looked into a room and found it empty and closed the door, only to open it a moment later and see the children, or some of them, half a dozen or so, sitting in a circle on the floor and twirling a bottle to see where it would point. They glanced up towards him and smiled, but paid no more attention to him than that; they preferred to watch the bottle slow and settle, to see whose turn it would be to accept the forfeit, if that was what the game involved. He might have asked, but something about their concentration dissuaded him. Eventually, he closed the door and walked away, and it seemed to him that there was silence once more; even the soft dry rattle of the glass against the wood could be heard no more.

Another afternoon, he had been staring at the empty lawn from a first-floor window for minutes on end, in a sort of trance; then, he must have blinked, he supposed later, but that one blink was time enough for the children to appear, as Melissa apparently had, and to be waving up. That was the other thing; they were at once aware of him, as though they had come back specifically, perhaps to reassure him that they were there. Which was quite the opposite of the effect their coming had.

Engel was another matter. Although he himself had observed how the children appeared to come and go at will, the notion that fleshy full-bodied Engel might do the same was inconceivable to the Doctor; to such an extent that he decided one day to take her into his confidence.

"You know what our friend Morgan thinks?" he said. They were both in the kitchen. Engel was making tea the way she liked it, strong and left to stew a little. The Doctor was warming his hands before the fire.

"Some nonsense, I suppose," she said, with affection. This was how they spoke of him when they were together, as though he were capable only of mischief.

"Well, yes, perhaps," he said. "It's hard to say. I thought so at first, but now I'm not so sure."

"That's got me curious," she said. She poured the tea out into large white mugs, added sugar and a splash of whisky.

Crane took a deep breath, then began. "He says the children seem to disappear sometimes, when they're not with us, when they're not being watched by anyone. I think he's beginning to wonder if they're really here at all.

Perhaps he's invented them, that's what he thinks, though he didn't say that, quite. He wouldn't." He stirred his mug slowly and sipped, then blew on the tea to cool it down, before sipping again. When he had finished this, he said, "That's what he's afraid of, I think, discovering that they're figments of his imagination. They come through the air, he said. I think he wonders sometimes if he might have made them up. Which would mean that he was mad."

"And you?" said Engel. "What do you think?"

Doctor Crane sipped again, and blew.

"I don't think he's mad," he said after a moment.

"Nor I," said Engel, "I don't think he's got an ounce of madness in him, though he'd have the right to it."

"So I suppose I may believe him," he said.

Engel nodded and drank. "He's no madman," she said again. "He's as sane as I am. Saner."

"But it isn't possible, surely?" the Doctor said, conscious that he was behaving in a manner that might seem peculiar to anyone else, asking the housekeeper for what amounted to a medical opinion, yet unable to do otherwise. "That the children come and go?"

"They're bright enough," she said. "They're bright as buttons, even the babies. Who knows what they can do?"

"But what are they here for, do you think?" the Doctor said.

Engel smiled.

# CHAPTER ELEVEN

in which David learns to read

It was true that the Doctor was studying. Soon after they had passed the first few afternoons of backgammon together, Morgan had begun to show him round the garden and then the house. He had taken him to the other three floors, long corridors giving onto barely furnished rooms. The Doctor had lingered in one of these rooms, crossing to the window and looking out towards the hills. "I should like to have this room," he said and immediately Morgan had told him that it was his. "You know this whole house is yours," he said, hearing his voice break, aware for the first time that he had made a friend or, rather, that *they* had each made friends, of each other. "I don't want the house," said Crane, with a smile. "I mean the freedom of it," replied Morgan. "Yes, that I have," said the Doctor, "and I'm more than grateful for it. But I would like this room for mine. I would like to work here, you see, where I can see the hills." He pointed towards them. "That's where I come from, my family, that is. We lived over there until my father died." Morgan followed the man's forefinger with his eyes, half expecting to find a house, the house in which Crane's family might have lived, but all he could see was the blue-grey line of the hills, beyond the garden and the wall and the woods that lay behind it. He had never been there, he had barely been more than twenty miles from the house in all his life, apart from occasional visits to the city with his father and his time in the clinic, and he had no idea where that was, although he had sometimes wondered. He might have asked Crane, who would surely have known; but they had never spoken again about his face, not after that first time. He had thought as he lay in his bed in the clinic that the hardest thing would be pain, but he had been wrong, he realized soon enough, as nurses came and went with their slop bowls and trays of implements and specialists took frozen-faced visitors from bed to bed. The thing that most abased him, that most abased them all, was pity. Crane had understood that. He talked to Morgan's face as indifferently as the children did.

"What kind of work do you expect to do?" Morgan said.

Crane looked excited. "Well," he replied, "you have so many books here. Rooms full of books that you haven't even begun to catalogue. Not just the ones in the library, or in your room, though, God knows, there are more than enough there. I walk around and it's endless. Books I would guess you've never even seen. I was rooting around a few days ago and I found a pile of old medical books, herbariums, works of anatomy, half of them not even in English, in French and German; some of them seemed to be in Arabic, though what I shall make of those I don't know. It struck me that I could look through them to see what they say. You never know what I might find. I might be no more than a family doctor, but I haven't stopped *wondering*." He rubbed his large red hands together and grinned like a boy. Morgan nodded.

"They were my grandfather's books, all of them," he said. "There are hundreds, maybe thousands, of books about medicine, mostly, and a hundred other things. My grandfather

wondered too, you see. I'll have them brought here for you."
And over the next few days the gardeners carried trunks of
books to Crane's room.

As Crane darted among the trunks, he discovered that
David wanted to learn to read. The first few days the boy
seemed content to sit in the room, on a small chair he had
found somewhere else in the house and carried there himself,
quietly watching the Doctor arrange the books in one bookcase
and then another. Later, as Crane settled into an armchair,
with the boy beside him, he became aware that David was
leaning forward and moving his lips, not uttering a sound, as
though he were reading the words on the page of Crane's book
to himself. The book was written in French, a language the
Doctor understood, but with difficulty, and he realized that he
was silently mouthing the words as he read, as though listening
to himself. David must have thought that reading was that, a
sort of silent listening. He closed the book.

"Would you like to learn to read?" he said.

"Is that what you're doing?" David said. "Are you reading
now?"

The Doctor nodded.

"Then, yes, I would," said David, with a shy smile, as
though he had just been offered a slice of cake or a special
treat of some kind. He took the Doctor's hand and squeezed
it tightly, so that Crane was unexpectedly moved. "Can you
show me how to do it? So that I can help you."

"Help me?"

"Yes."

"Help me to do what?"

"To find what you're looking for."

"And what's that, do you think?" the Doctor asked,

amused, but also curious. "What am I looking for, do you think?" But David didn't answer. The Doctor reached for a book in English and opened it to the first page. There was a picture of a plant on the left and, on the right, a description of the plant. The book was old but not too old, he thought. He pointed to the name of the plant, *arnica*, and pronounced the word, and then the first letter, *a*. "Yes, yes," said David, nodding in an anxious, impatient way, "I see. I mean, I understand."

"Repeat it then," the Doctor said.

David learned quickly. Sometimes the Doctor felt that the boy was not so much learning to read as remembering a skill he had momentarily lost. His eyes would move down the page with a hungry expression, as though in search of something, even as his lips pronounced the words above. He began to choose the books he wanted to learn from, in a way that made no immediate sense to the Doctor. Not all were books he would have chosen to teach a child his letters, but that didn't matter to David. If the Doctor hesitated, David sat there and waited, unbudgeable. Soon, within days, it seemed, David was reading alone, taking the books he had chosen to a small chair on the other side of the room. That was when he asked the Doctor if he could teach the others to read, all of them, even the youngest. Even the babies, he seemed to mean.

"Why don't you show Morgan what you've learned first?" Crane said after a moment, wanting to see what David would say. "I'm sure he'll be so pleased."

David looked doubtful.

"But I want it to be a surprise," he said, his lower lip jutting out in a gesture so petulant, so childish, that Crane noticed, as he had done before, how rarely David behaved like a child.

"It will be a surprise," Crane said. "I haven't breathed a word to him of this. He thinks I'm studying on my own account."

"No," said David, shaking his head. "Not the reading. I didn't mean the reading." And then he looked anxious, as though he had said too much, and regretted it. He thought for a moment, then came to a decision.

"All right," the boy said.

"What did you mean, David, by a surprise?" Crane said, his curiosity too strong to be suppressed. "What did you want to be a surprise?"

David closed his book and grinned. The Doctor was startled. David was generally such a solemn boy.

"It doesn't matter," he said. "It will be in any case." Placing the book he was holding back on the shelf, he ran from the room. The Doctor heard him calling to the others, wherever they were. It was true that they seemed to disappear, as Morgan had said, only to reappear when summoned. This time it was David who had done the summoning.

He didn't teach them all, of course; the babies were far too young and some of the others seemed to show no interest. He chose the two girls nearest to him in age, Daisy and Melissa. It was odd and wonderful to watch the three of them as they sat together in a row on a sofa beneath the window; the Doctor's room was gradually being filled with furniture. David would sit in the middle and trace the word with his finger, his voice so low that Crane could hardly hear him, while the voices of the girls, less certain, picked up and repeated what he said. At times, David took one of their fingers in his hand and held it to a word, and it seemed to the Doctor that the girl, who was usually Daisy, could see the word more clearly once she had touched the letters, repeating it in a stronger voice and with greater confidence than before. It was odd because they were all so young, but once that sense of oddness had passed, there was nothing more natural than for the three small heads to be bent together over a book of medicine written a hundred years before. Crane watched the way David treated the girls. With Daisy, he was cautious, gentle, eager to help when she was discouraged. Melissa, though, he treated as an equal and Crane observed that within a week she was reading as easily as David. Watching them together, he saw a likeness between them grow, or his awareness of it did, until they looked like twins. He said this to Morgan one day.

"It's interesting that you should say that. She seemed to know him when she arrived," Morgan said. "Come to that, she seemed to know us all. She ran to me, I remember, I picked her up and she kissed my cheek." And he lifted his hand to touch where the kiss had been. "There are times I think they were all together before they came here, wherever they were, wherever that was. Some other place."

"They're learning to read, you know."

Morgan was surprised.

"Really? Was that your idea?"

The Doctor shook his head. "Not at all. It was David's. Now he's teaching the girls. Melissa and Daisy. And some of the smaller ones too. Jules, I think, the little dark-eyed one. The two who are always holding hands and won't be separated. I find it impossible to believe, yet it's also the most natural thing in the world. You should see them; I'd take you there now, except that I think they'd be annoyed with me for having told you. They want it to be a surprise, I think, though I'm not sure that I've understood correctly." He smiled. "David's a mystery, as you know."

"Where do they do it?" Morgan asked.

"Wherever they happen to be," said the Doctor. "Sometimes they sit in a circle in my room with me, while I work. I've seen them in the garden too. I wouldn't be surprised if they didn't go to the kitchen sometimes; I don't know if Engel has seen them or not, I haven't asked her; but I wouldn't be surprised. These days, David's never without a book. It's as though he were always ready. I think their favourite place is the stairs going up to the first floor. They sit on the top steps, just below the landing, in rows, like mice. You can almost imagine their tails curling behind them." The Doctor was amused by this picture he had made.

"Do you think I should pretend not to know?" Morgan said.

"I don't see why you should. Perhaps you could stumble on them one morning. It shouldn't be that difficult. I'm surprised you haven't caught them at it yourself."

"Because I should like them to have a special place to go to do these things," Morgan said thoughtfully. "They could use the room that used to be my schoolroom if they wanted. It would be nice to think that it might finally serve some purpose."

What Morgan imagined was a vision of the great house like a constellation, with each of the special rooms like a star. There was his book room, where he would read and play backgammon with the Doctor; there was the room of the

Doctor himself, from which you could see the distant hills of his childhood; perhaps at the heart of the constellation was Engel's kitchen, which smelt of coffee and rising dough; now, and this seemed more right to him the more he considered it, there would be the schoolroom, his schoolroom.

# CHAPTER TWELVE

*in which a box reveals its secret and Morgan is moved*

The Doctor was searching through boxes in the dusty attics one day for any more books that might serve his purpose, when he came across a large chest placed vertically against the back wall of one of the many rooms. It was made of finely embossed leather, the colour of dried blood, with brass hoops circling it and a brace of large brass padlocks and other attachments the purpose of which wasn't clear. He tried to open the first padlock and found that, though closed, it had not been locked. He slipped off both this padlock and the next and opened the lid, which—given the upright position of the chest—was more like a door, then stepped back with a startled cry. Inside the chest was a human figure. Overcoming his surprise, he approached the chest a second time and saw that the figure's two sides, being hinged, could be folded back to reveal the incomplete form of a pregnant woman, naked, with an elaborate hairstyle and carefully painted face. The figure was cut off at the lower thighs, so that the woman's face was barely above the level of his navel. It was hard to see what she was made of, primarily because the effect was so convincing; his instinct told him she had been fashioned from living flesh. There was perhaps a gleam to her which suggested the use of polish, yet her skin gave the impression of being warm to the touch, to such a degree that Crane was seized by an odd reluctance to let his hand rest on the woman's head. Her hair had been twisted into a rope and braided with ribbons before being bound around her head in a style that was both prim and ornate. Her lips were vermilion, her eyes dark brown, her face a pallid olive. The skin on the rest of her body was milk-white; it was an antique body in that it had never been exposed to the sun. Her hands were fine and covered with jewels set in rings, which seemed to be real. She had an amber at her neck, set in an intricate web of gold, which emphasized her nakedness. Inside the amber was the hollowed-out carcass of a bee. Aware that he was behaving foolishly, he summoned his nerve and touched the woman's cheek with the tips of his fingers.

"She's beautiful," said David. The Doctor froze, then whipped his hand away.

"How long have you been there?" he said, spinning round, his tone harsher than he would have liked. He felt that he had been caught in some wrongdoing. But David didn't seem to have noticed Crane's embarrassment. He was standing with Melissa and one of the babies, the Doctor wasn't sure which one, beneath the lowest point of the roof that allowed him not to crouch. Melissa had the baby against her breast.

"Oh, ages," David said. He took the Doctor's hand in his, guiding it back towards the woman. They touched the face together as Melissa and the baby joined them. It was smooth and cool, quite unlike flesh as it turned out; more like porcelain, thought the Doctor. The baby made a low chortling noise.

"Where is she from?" David said.

"I don't know."

"She's beautiful," David said again. "Isn't she, Melissa?"

"Yes," said Melissa, whispering this word into the baby's ear.

"And she's got no clothes on at all," said David, to the Doctor this time. "Why's that?"

"I think she's a model someone must have made so that people can see her body and the baby inside it," the Doctor said. "Look here, at her tummy, do you see? She's going to have a baby at any minute," he said. He examined her body more closely and saw that the nipples had been modelled as finely as the rest, the dark brown areolae stippled with tiny bumps, the painted trace of a hair. But it was only when he ran his hand down her massively distended belly, startled by the unexpected *warmth* of it, that he felt what he might never have seen with the naked eye.

"Well I never," he said. "There's a join here. Look at this, David. Just look at this. There's a kind of seam." As he spoke he pressed the palm of his hand against the surface of the woman's belly. There was a faint click from deep within the figure and the belly opened like a split fruit to reveal, on one side, what would have been the flesh of the fruit beneath the peel and, on the other side, what would have been the kernel. The flesh was a cushion of fat and veins. The kernel was a curled fetus, the head pressed low against the neck of the womb, the fetus almost, but not quite, an actual child. Part of the placenta had been left across a section of the fetus, like a meaty veil. The Doctor reached down between the woman's legs and found the vagina dilated. Melissa had put the living baby down on the floor so that she could kneel to see better. Before anyone could stop her, she had crawled as near to the woman as she could get and touched the spot the Doctor's hand had touched. He saw the baby's tiny fingers enter and reappear beside the head of the fetus, the baby's wrist encircled by the vagina of the woman. The baby caressed the head of the fetus with the tips of her fingers and then withdrew her hand and turned to Melissa, who smiled and nodded.

The position of the woman's hands and arms reminded the Doctor of something. Her right hand was raised, palm facing out; her left hand was extended, the palm turned up and slightly cupped, as if to make an offering. That was it; she looked like a votive statue, the kind that was used in ancient Greece. Yet the detail of the fetus and veins, the blood vessels and the folds of the vagina, the overall accuracy of the modelling made it clear that her function was also to describe the female body, to inform and explain herself to others. She reminded him of something else, something he had seen recently. In one of the books in his room, perhaps. Yes, that was it. Moving the baby away a little, despite her protests, he closed the woman's belly around the fetus and then, for safety's sake, the chest around the woman.

The children followed him as he ran downstairs towards his study. He was almost at the door when he noticed Morgan at a window at the far end of the corridor. He must have been waiting, the Doctor thought. "Come here," he shouted. "I've got something to show you." By the time Morgan was in the room, the Doctor had pulled out half a dozen books and was rifling through them, as though he was scared he might forget what he was looking for before he had found it. Morgan stood with the three children, David, Melissa, and the baby, while the Doctor picked up one book and put it down, then picked up another and did the same, increasingly frustrated. "I know I've seen her somewhere," he muttered to himself. Morgan sank down on his knees until his one good eye was level with David, who did not flinch.

"What's going on?" he said.

"We've found a woman with a baby inside her," David said. "She was in a box in the attic."

Morgan stood up smartly. "What do you mean, a woman with a baby inside her? A dead woman? A baby? What kind of story is this?" He glanced at the Doctor with unexpected irritation, as though he had been let down. David looked momentarily hurt.

"No, no," laughed the Doctor, as though nothing could be less likely. "A model of a woman, made of wax I think although I'm not quite sure, but an absolute cracker. An authentic beauty. Italian, I'd put money on it. Hang on a second until I've found what I'm looking for, it must be here somewhere, and I'll show you." He darted across to his desk. "I know I've seen her recently, in this room, in one of these blessed books," he said, pulling out a large flat volume, rather like an atlas, from beneath a pile of others, which tottered and fell to the floor. Melissa put the baby down and started to pick them up, while the Doctor flipped the pages of this large book over, balancing it clumsily in the crook of his other arm. "Yes, here she is, I knew it!" he cried. "Here she is, my lovely." He held the book open to show to the others, as much to David as to Morgan.

They saw an engraving, coloured by hand, of the woman in the box upstairs. The belly was closed tight in the picture, but the Doctor turned the page, struggling to hold the book up as he did so, and there she was again, the same calm face and perfect hair, her belly opened like a nut and the fetus visible. The Doctor turned the book back round and glanced at the caption. "It's the work of an Italian," he said, "three hundred years ago, in Florence. And I was right, she is made of wax, of dyed and painted wax. But what an artist! And what a man of science!" The Doctor slammed the book shut and ran towards the door. "Don't just stand there, Morgan! Come on!" he cried, and ran from the room. The others followed him and, as they hurried in single file along the corridor, it seemed to Morgan that all the other children must have been waiting behind doors for them to pass because the stairs that led up to the attic were immediately filled with children, some of them walking on their own, others being carried or pulled by the older ones, in a buzz of excited chatter. By the time they had reached the attic room in which the woman was kept, the entire household, with the exception of Engel, had gathered around the two men, the smallest babies lying on the floor in front of them, the toddlers seated behind. The Doctor opened the door of the chest and then, as though silence could be deeper than itself, the air of the room seemed to empty as the Doctor opened the perfect belly of the waxen woman to reveal the fetus within. Nobody moved a muscle until Morgan passed through the children, who shuffled and edged to one side to make room for him. He touched the woman's cheek with the back of his hand.

"It must have been my grandfather," he said. "My grandfather must have found her on his travels and had her shipped here."

"I was right, you see," Doctor Crane said behind him.

"She is Italian. You can see that from her face, her colouring, the way her hair has been arranged. She's like a woman from a painting."

Morgan's good hand slid down the cheek of the woman onto her chin, resting for a second on the bone between her breasts, his fingers brushing the husk of the bee in the amber drop, then further down until they came to the edge of the part that had been opened to reveal the fetus.

"No, not like this, not like this, so bare and cruel," he said under his breath, and closed the woman's belly with his other hand, the damaged one, pushing until he heard the click within. She was closed to him now, and whole. He stroked her pale distended skin as tears poured down his cheeks.

"What on earth's the matter?" Doctor Crane said.

"I don't know," said Morgan. "I wish I did." When Doctor Crane put his arm round Morgan's shoulder and pulled the man in towards him, so that his wounded face would rest on the taller man's chest, Morgan began to cry as he had never cried before, not even as a child; he cried until he was utterly drained. The children around them were silent and observing, but happily so, as though they had known this would happen in the end, and were glad. Finally, Morgan broke away, although a hand remained on the Doctor's waist.

"Well," he said, and gave a short embarrassed laugh. "It seems I am an emotional creature."

# CHAPTER THIRTEEN

*in which Doctor Crane enquires about Morgan's sister*
*and Morgan wonders about the nature of power*

One day, soon after the woman had been discovered, David asked Morgan about his sister.

"How do you know I've got a sister? Did Engel tell you?"

David shrugged. "I know you've got a sister," he insisted, "but I don't know her name."

After a moment, because Morgan had almost forgotten his sister's name he thought of her so rarely, he said, "She's called Rebecca."

"Why did she go away from here?"

"She's never really been here, not since she was a child. She went away to school, you see, while I was educated at home." Why am I telling this to David? he wondered. Why should he need to know? Morgan had no desire to talk about his sister, but he could see that David would insist; his small bright features were set with determination. He would have to talk. He closed his eyes for a second as if to think, although he was mostly trying not to think. "She went away and she stayed away, really. When my mother was ill, she hardly ever visited, whether through her own choice or not I couldn't say. At Christmas perhaps. I saw her at my father's funeral. She's taller than I am, tall and blond, a striking woman. We aren't alike at all. I don't think I've seen her since then, though I know she visited me in hospital. She saw me, you see, and then she went."

David wasn't interested in this. "What does she do?" he said.

"Do? She works in the family business, I believe. There are letters sometimes, things to sign. She sends them and I sign them and send them back."

"She's important there?"

"Well, yes, I suppose she must be running the entire show. She's the owner, after all, along with me, and I have no interest at all, I have never had any interest in the family business. After my father's death, there was a manager, like a regent, who took over until my sister was old enough, but he must be retired by now. Rebecca always liked being in charge, I remember that. I think that was why my mother didn't like her." His mother had always disliked Rebecca even as a child. He saw his sister in his mind's eye. A stubborn, hard-featured child with short fair hair tugged back from her face and tied with ribbon into a single clump that would gradually work itself free. Small plump hands clenched by her side. Hating her mother back.

"What is she like now?" said David. "I mean, is she good?"

"Good?" said Morgan. He considered this for a moment. "I've no idea. I don't know her, you see, David. I've never thought of her as good, or not good, for that matter. I don't know how those words work when I think of her. Good, bad." He remembered that he was talking to a child. "I suppose goodness depends on what you do, as much as what you are. I think she may have sent Engel here to look after me, when I most needed to be looked after. That would have been a good thing for her to do." So perhaps she is good, he said to himself.

David shook his head. "Engel isn't here for you," he said. He stood for a moment, in thought, before speaking again. "What does your family business do?" he said.

"Do?" Morgan hadn't expected this question.

"Yes." David sounded impatient now. He stamped his foot. "What does it do? It must do something. *Make* something, I don't know."

"Yes, it does," said Morgan. "It makes power."

David nodded.

"That's what I hoped," he said. He thought again. "Where does power come from, Morgan?" he said finally.

"Gas. Coal. The sun," said Morgan.

"No, not that kind of power," said David. "The other kind."

"What other kind?"

"I've been reading books," said David, in a long-suffering way, as though no explanation were really needed. "The kind of power that kings have, and Caesars."

Morgan considered this. "From the strength of others, I suppose," he said finally. "By stealing it from them and making it your own."

David nodded, as if a suspicion had been confirmed, and walked off to look for the others.

Morgan brooded about this conversation for some time after David had left him. Not the power part, other than to smile to himself at David's precociousness, but the part about Engel. If Engel wasn't there for him, to meet his needs, then who *was* she there for? The children? Who else, if not? She must have been waiting for them to arrive, caring for him as a way of passing the time until the moment came for her to fulfill her role. But his sister? Did his sister know about the children? How much did Rebecca know about his life here? About the Doctor? How much did Rebecca know about their daily business in this house that was also hers, although she never came and had never loved it, as far as he could remember. Why should she? It has never been a house that welcomed love, he thought. And then he heard shouting rise up from the garden, children's voices, and laughter. He crossed the room and looked down towards the lawn, where David and some of the smaller ones were chasing a ball. Not until now.

He observed them, unaware of the passage of time, until he felt a chill in the air from the opened window and saw the children run back into the house in a group, the ball forgotten until David paused, turned back to pick it up. Morgan watched the boy stand with the ball beneath his arm and look towards the lake, and the boathouse. He seemed to be waiting for a sign, or seeking one out, some sign that would have meaning only for him, thought Morgan. He stepped back into the room, shaken by some feeling he could not name. When he stepped forward and looked down once again towards the garden, David was no longer there.

# CHAPTER FOURTEEN

*in which the children lose their temper and make a discovery*

The children sat in a huddle on the floor of the Doctor's room, books scattered around them, some open, some closed, in terrible disorder. It hurt the Doctor to see books treated in such a way. They're too young for this, he thought, all at once. And then, as though this had never occurred to him before, because it remained unanswered and so was always new, there were the usual questions in his head: Who *are* they? What do they want? Today, something curious was going on, that was clear. David and Melissa, normally so equable, so *adult* in their dealings with the world, even inscrutably so, seemed angry, as much with the smaller ones as with themselves, while Daisy, seated a little apart from the others on a footstool near his armchair, crooned to one of the babies, her face turned away.

"What's wrong?" said the Doctor.

"It isn't here," said David in a rage that bordered on tantrum, beating the book on his lap with his small tight fist. "That's what. We can't find it. We've looked and looked in all these books and it isn't anywhere to be found." He stared up at the Doctor, his face contorted by fury. The Doctor had seen nothing like it in any of the children. "But it must be. It must be here somewhere," the boy said, throwing the book down and picking up another. "Or what's the point?"

"But what?" said the Doctor. "What are you looking for that's so important?"

"What we were looking for," insisted Melissa when David didn't answer. "That's what's important."

"But what is it, this thing that's so important?" the Doctor said, all at once exasperated. "Perhaps if you tell me I can help you look for it. I might even know where it is."

"They won't know till they find it," said Daisy in a voice that was both petulant and resigned. "No one will. That's what they say. But they make me look all the same. I think it's silly."

"*We* won't know," said David, glancing at Daisy with fury, as though she had blabbed some secret. "*You* won't know, you mean. *None* of us will know. You're not so special that you don't have work to do just like the rest of us. That's why we're here."

Melissa stood up and walked across to the other little girl.

"We've got it wrong, I think," she said. "We must have made a mistake somehow. It must be our fault." She touched Daisy's hair. "Don't worry. We'll find it, I know we will. And then we can all go home."

"I'm not worried," said Daisy, turning her head, and the Doctor saw that she had been crying. Daisy was his favourite among the children, perhaps because she had been the first to need him. But more than that, what appealed to him most—what made him feel safe with her was the truth of it, although he didn't know this or wouldn't admit it to himself, because why should he, of all people, feel insecure?—was her normality. She seemed like any other child. She seemed to know nothing more than she should. But what was it that Melissa had said? *Go home?*

"What on earth do you mean?" he said.

She stared up at him, her expression almost hostile, as though she had been surprised in the middle of something shameful and refused to be ashamed, as though it were the Doctor, not she, who should feel shame for having been overcurious or indiscreet. Appalled, he felt the urge to step back, to get away from this child with her soft blond curls and green eyes and lips set accusingly in a line. *Who are these children?* he asked himself. *What do they want?*

Then David stood up as well and took the Doctor's hand. "Doctor Crane, come with me now, I have found something," he said, and his face broke into a smile that made the Doctor more uneasy than ever. "Please," the boy insisted in an uncharacteristic wheedling tone. The Doctor looked questioningly at Melissa as David pulled him towards the door. "Come on!" the boy insisted, tugging at the Doctor's hand with both of his, and there was something in his voice that reminded the Doctor of his own voice, of when he had also said these words a week or so before. He wondered as they walked together from the room and down the corridor to where the stairs led up to the attic, the boy leading the man, the others following, how much of what the children said had not been said to them, how much of what they did was not the simulacrum of what had been done around them. Their perfection, it seemed to the Doctor, because they were all undeniably quite perfect, was like the perfection of the woman made of wax.

David took them from the room in which the woman remained in her upright trunk and through another series of rooms until they were at the centre of the house. There were boxes and dust and more boxes; empty clothes rails had been stacked against the farthest wall, and covered in sheets. There was no light apart from a thin stream that came in where a tile or two had been dislodged; beneath it, in correspondence, was a patch of damp. Light and water. Water and light.

David had found a large black torch from somewhere. He turned it on and balanced it on a box, then crossed the room and hauled out an ancient pram from behind one of the clothes rails. The Doctor shivered as David reached into the pram and gathered something in his arms. The children sighed with pleasure and the Doctor gave a short, involuntary cry, like a bark, which sounded to him as though it had come from someone else, from somewhere close by.

David was clutching a severed head to his chest. The head was natural size and larger than David's own, because it had belonged to a fully grown man. The face was pressed against David's body; all that could be seen was the carefully arranged coal-black hair, curling into the nape, and the intricate pattern of vein and artery and bone in the neck, like a slice of polished marble as it glinted in the light of the torch. There was a sheen to it, it looked almost wet; it might have been freshly cut, the Doctor thought, bending down to see better. It might have been the head of a victim of some terror from the past, the head of an innocent or guilty man from a time when innocence and guilt were meaningless and the blade fell where it fell. Then David turned the head round and the Doctor saw the face of a man that might have been the brother of the pregnant woman, so strong was the resemblance, and understood at once that this was the work of the same creator, the wax artist, the surgeon.

"You found this here?" he said. David nodded. He put the head down beside the torch, but the Doctor touched his shoulder.

"We can see it better if we take it to another room, where there's more light," he said. David picked up the head and nodded a second time.

The Doctor led the way through the attic rooms until they were in a space with skylights. He could have taken them all downstairs to his own room, but felt, superstitiously he knew, that the head belonged up here, with the pregnant woman, returned to her trunk until Morgan had decided what he would do with her. Morgan was fascinated and disturbed by her in equal measure. When she was closed and whole, he wanted her open; when she was open and exposed, he could barely look at her without reaching forward to touch the fetus, the glistening wave of placenta. Then, with a shudder, he would swing the flap of belly shut and turn away, the colour drained from his face. "Let's leave it where we found it," Crane had said and Morgan, in an angry whisper, had insisted: "Her."

They stopped and David put the head down on a table beneath one of the skylights, where it could be seen by everyone. The Doctor stood beside him, the other children forming a ragged circle around the two. David rotated the head slowly until it had been seen by everyone, smiling when some of the smaller children giggled nervously. "There's nothing to be afraid of," he said. "Is there, Doctor?"

"No," said the Doctor, crouching down to examine

the head more closely. "Nothing at all." He looked at the eyes, which were made of glass, he imagined, nut-brown, the irises flecked with red and black, and the lashes, surely human, applied with infinite care to the wax. The cheeks were flushed and the full lips ribbed as finely as those of a child, almost adhesive in their moistness. The chin had the faintest suggestion of stubble, as though numerous grains of beard had been needled beneath the final layer of wax.

He was close enough to kiss it when David performed his final trick of the morning and the face swung away from the head, grazing the face of the Doctor, who leapt back, startled, even unnerved. "You see," the boy said with a tone of pride, "with the woman you can see the baby; here you can see the bones and then the brain." He touched the back of the head a second time and the front of the skull gave a shudder and then detached itself from the head as the face had done. At this point, the Doctor lost his caution and was simply awed. "What workmanship," he marvelled. "Look," said David, moving the bone layer back into place, "the nose isn't part of the head at all. It's only on the face. Beneath it there's a sort of hole. And look at the eyes. They join up here. You can't tell anything until it's open."

The Doctor thought of the time the artist must have spent with the dead to know such things. He closed up the head and then opened it, astonished by the clocklike precision of the hinges, which seemed to have been made of brass and, but for the central pin, were deeply embedded into the wax. When the head was closed, there was a person, his eyes, his mouth, a person who might have lived as he lived and have seen and spoken and heard as he did; then, one layer down, the hard unfeeling shell that outlives the rest and is indistinguishable at first glance from a hundred thousand others, the underlying oneness; and, finally, coiled grey matter, the workings of which are all that survive, beyond bone and expression, when the brain that thought and the skull that held the brain are equally gone to dust. But that's not guaranteed, thought the Doctor, not anymore; that even the workings of the brain will last more than the time it takes to tell them is no foregone conclusion.

# CHAPTER FIFTEEN

in which Morgan questions Doctor Crane
and the idea of movement is considered

It was David's discovery, so it seemed only fitting that David should decide when Morgan would see the head. Not yet, he told the Doctor. Not yet. Then, in a tone that amused the Doctor, coming from a child of—what would David be now?—ten? he had the mind of a ten-year-old, that was certain, yet might have been younger, must have been younger, in this knowing, portentous tone that seemed so inappropriate, he said, "The time will come. You'll see." It didn't occur to any of them how curious it was that Morgan should never be the discoverer himself; that his own house should remain so mysterious to him. While the others rooted and ferreted, the Doctor in one way and the children in another, Morgan would sit in his book room and wonder what the world he had made for himself might mean; or rather, what the world that had formed itself around him might want from him. Because that was where its meaning, and by extension his, would finally lie; in the demands it made on him. Sometimes it came to him that there was that other larger world the Doctor had described, that encircled the garden as the garden encircled him, and he wondered why his grandfather's house had been passed over and why he had been left alone. Was it possible that the wall was enough?

He would have pestered the Doctor for more detail if some foreboding hadn't stopped him, perhaps the fear that the Doctor would know something shameful and refuse to tell him, to protect him perhaps. He imagined himself the dirty secret at the heart of the world, the overlooked madwoman raving in the attic of a house that occupied everything there was, each brick and pane and board, the wondering prince in the hair-filled mask of iron he had dreamt of as a boy and never been able to forget.

But he still asked other questions.

"When you're away from here, away from the house, I wonder, where do you go?" Morgan asked the Doctor one evening, after they had eaten and Engel had taken the children off to bed.

The Doctor shrugged. "I have a room," he said.

"And you leave it without worrying? Without wondering what might happen?"

"Worrying? Why should I be worrying?"

"But isn't it dangerous to leave a room alone?" said Morgan, wondering if he sounded as foolish as he felt. Yet he had had this conversation with himself that afternoon and everything had made perfect sense. Perhaps he had overrehearsed. He wasn't sure in any case why this mattered so much to him, this life the Doctor might have away from the house, which by now he hardly left, except once a week, for half a day, when Morgan supposed he saw his other patients, because surely there would be others who needed the Doctor's care, out there, in that other world. Apart from that single afternoon each week, the Doctor was here in the house with them all. Sometimes, they passed so much time together, Morgan had the impression that his own body had been miraculously doubled, or split in half, and that beside him was the Doctor.

Sometimes he thought of himself as the Doctor.

"Rooms are never alone," said the Doctor with a laugh. "Only the people who live in them can be alone. I am alone, perhaps, in mine." He paused. "But you shouldn't worry on my behalf. There is nothing in my room in the city that matters to me in the slightest. It is quite bare. A bed, a desk, a chair. Even the window gives onto a painted brick wall only feet away. I always thought I liked the idea of living in a cell. I thought it appealed to the monk in me, because I admired the idea of vocation, you see, my father gave me that. But now, when I think of how I lived there, day after day, for almost four years in the end, I see that it didn't appeal to the monk in me at all, but to the convict. I was a prisoner there, in the bareness, and that was what appealed to me." He smiled. "But now I am a free man, Morgan. Besides, I would never have been a satisfactory convict. Convicts leave their mark as often and as deeply as they can."

"I should like to see it," Morgan said, in a tone that struck them both as stubborn and contrary, although to what wasn't clear; as though his wishes were being opposed.

"If you wish. I could take you there if you like."

But the sudden willingness in the Doctor's voice had a strange effect on Morgan. "I didn't mean that I should like to leave the grounds," he snapped.

"Yet there's no earthly reason why you shouldn't," the Doctor said in a low voice.

"No earthly reason," repeated Morgan. Crane said no more. Soon after this conversation, Morgan heard him leave the house. He heard Crane's car start up, its wheels move briefly against the gravel. He is going back to his cell in the city, Morgan thought, to his narrow monk's bed. I have disappointed him, he thought. Without Crane, with the children in bed, there was silence.

He had always loved silence, the blanket of it, but the children bridled against it, as children do. They would wait for him to leave the room before beginning their racket once more, their shouting and sparring and rearranging of objects, to what purpose he didn't know; perhaps there was no purpose, he would think, and be proved wrong. He imagined the willful destruction of toys and board games, child-sized pieces of furniture, only to find, when he investigated their cupboards and boxes at night and he could wander at will around the house, that everything was whole and in its place. They left no mark, other than those in his silence, dents and bruises on the surface of that frail receptacle into which he had always withdrawn, and in which he no longer found any comfort.

That night, when Morgan couldn't sleep for thinking, he heard a muffled rustling in the corridor outside his room. He lay there for a while, alert to what might be there, which seemed both light and numerous. It was hard to tell if the noise were produced by limbs or voices; it sounded like a mixture of whispering and shuffling; a leisurely ruffle of wings perhaps. He would have opened the door to see, but that would have had the unwanted effect of bringing the noise, which had begun to have the form of music, to an end. Movement, he thought, that's what it takes. I am being reminded of movement.

# CHAPTER SIXTEEN

in which the car is prepared for service

A few days later Morgan sent a note with Daisy to the head gardener.

"What does it say?" she said.

"Open it, my dear, and read it, if you like," Morgan said. Daisy opened the note.

"It says Dear Mr. Green I would be grateful if you would see what can be done to ensure that my father's car is repaired and restored to full working order. No expense need be spared. Please inform me of your progress as soon as is reasonable," read Daisy. She looked up. "Is that the old car in the garage with the cloth all over it? The one that's been banged in at the front? The one with the rats in it?"

"Yes."

"But what do you want it for?" she said. She sounded anxious.

"Wouldn't you like to be driven round the grounds in my father's car?" Morgan said. "It used to be a very fine car indeed, the best that money could buy. My father was proud of it. Who knows, maybe one day we could even go for a ride outside," he added, as though this thought had just that moment occurred to him. But Daisy didn't seem to be impressed.

"Have you told David you want to use the car?" she said in a low voice, hardly more than a whisper.

Morgan laughed. "Now why on earth should I tell David?" he said. "You think I should first ask David for permission?"

Daisy hung her head, but didn't speak.

"Run along now and take my note to Mr. Green, and then come back and tell me what he says," Morgan said after a moment. He watched the little girl as she ran down the garden, then hurried to the kitchen in an odd mood, needing to talk to Engel. She was mincing horseradish, her round cheeks streaming with tears.

"Sometimes I wonder whose house this is," he said.

"I can't think why," said Engel.

"Yet it's true, I do wonder. For example, can you think of any reason why I should need to ask David before I do things?" he said in a tone that he had intended to be playful, but that sounded, to his ear and no doubt to Engel's, peeved.

"I don't know what you're talking about," said Engel in an impatient way. "You're the master here, you know that as well as I do. Needing to ask David!"

"I certainly believed that to be the case," Morgan said. "But now I find that David, of all people, has to be informed of my every move." He laughed, unconvinced, even hurt.

"I've never heard such nonsense," said Engel.

Morgan walked to the window and stared out. It had started to rain. There was no sign of anyone outside. Daisy would have found Mr. Green by now and delivered his note. Perhaps the gardener was standing in the garage now, with the damaged car in front of him, wondering where to start. Perhaps he had already begun to kill with his spade the rats that were nesting there. What had possessed him to ask for such a thing, wondered Morgan.

"Where is he?"

"David?" Engel sniffed. "He'll be about."

"Where does he go, do you think?"

Engel put down the ragged horseradish root and stepped back from the mincer, wiping her eyes on her apron.

"This horseradish makes me cry like no other thing in the world," she said.

"Where *does* he go, though?" Morgan repeated, as though to himself. "Where do they all go, come to that? Just listen. A houseful of children and not a sound."

"And you're complaining, my young man," she said, as she did when she was annoyed with him, perhaps unaware that he welcomed it. "You should have lived in a whole house the size of this kitchen with children that made themselves heard and seen, as I have done."

"No, not that. Not that at all." He blinked as the pungency of the root reached him. "I'm not complaining. I wonder, that's all it is."

"You listen to the Doctor," Engel said, with a trace of irritation. "He'll tell you what's what."

"Why? Have you spoken to the Doctor about this?" asked Morgan sharply. Engel turned her back on him.

"I'll not be questioned," she said coldly. "Not by you or by anyone. Not in that way. You have no right."

"Oh, Engel, please," said Morgan, horrified. Engel had never used this tone with him. "The last thing I would do is question you or do anything, anything, that might upset you. You know that, surely. You know that I depend on you absolutely."

"I know what I know," she said. Then, in a gentler manner, she added, "You just talk to the Doctor, that's all. He's the one you should talk to, not me."

But I have spoken to the Doctor and the Doctor knows nothing, thought Morgan, or will not tell me what he knows. And I still have no answer. Why *should* I have spoken to David? With a sense of fear he couldn't understand, he wondered, And what would David have said? Do I need David's consent before I do things? Who is he? What does he want from me? It struck him that the language David used had a religious quality to it. You couldn't get round it, or through it. It blocked you, that's all. It leaves you no choice. I wonder where they are now, he said to himself, and then the thought came to him that he would have this out with David. He would find him and talk to him, man-to-man. He left the kitchen and crossed the hall, almost running, fired by this idea. At the bottom of the stairs, he paused and listened, but could hear nothing above the sound of the rain, which was falling more heavily now, beating against the stone pathway around the house, striking the windowpanes. They must be inside the house, he thought, and began to climb the stairs.

They were seated in the schoolroom. He had never seen a room so full. There were children everywhere, so many he began to wonder if there were children in the house that he had never seen before, if new children had arrived without his having been told. But the impression of fullness was created by the room itself, by its size and by the memories he had of it, of its emptiness; the contrast of its emptiness. It did him good to see it filled like this.

Each head was bowed, he saw, above a sheet of white paper, with a book beneath it to serve as support, and poised above each sheet of paper was a small hand with a pen or pencil in it. Some of them surely were too young to be writing actual words, he thought, and imagined they were drawing, or mimicking their elders. He stepped a little closer, to see what they were doing. He was leaning over to examine the work of the nearest child, who happened to be Moira, when David spoke.

"We are writing," he said, in his patient adult's voice. "We need to be able to write, you see. Reading alone isn't enough. Writing's how things are passed on. Otherwise everything we know would die with us and be forgotten."

Morgan smiled. "Of course it is, David."

David pointed at a blackboard that Morgan hadn't seen before, its easel near the wall behind David's back. Morgan read the words that someone, presumably David, had written on the board, in yellow chalk. They'd been written in capital letters, to make them easier for little hands to copy, he supposed, but that only made their sense more awful. Morgan's hand rose to his mouth to stifle a cry. This is what they said:

I AM ONLY A CHILD BUT ALREADY
I HAVE UNDERSTOOD THE WICKEDNESS
OF THE WORLD.

# CHAPTER SEVENTEEN

in which Trilby and Pate return to the house

A few weeks after that, when the weather had turned for the worse, Trilby and Pate came back. They weren't alone this time. Morgan was wandering from his bedroom along the hall upstairs when he heard noises outside; engines being turned off, voices; he hurried across the landing to one of the windows that overlooked the drive. There were two black cars, both armoured, and a group of men beside them, among them Trilby and Pate. One of the men he didn't recognize had opened the back door of the larger car and was letting out a pair of dogs on leashes. For a moment he saw his mother's wolfhounds before him as the two grey dogs tugged towards the house, their mouths open; the stronger of the two began to bark and was whipped across the haunches with the loose end of a leash. Trilby and Pate were in suits, as they had been the first time, but the other men, five of them, were in a sort of uniform that meant nothing to Morgan, olive-green trousers and jackets, heavy boots, belts; one of them was black with ringlets of oiled hair to his shoulders, the others had blond hair shaved almost to the scalp. They all wore slim metal batons dangling from their waists. Hardly breathing, Morgan watched Trilby take off his hat and wipe his forehead on his sleeve before replacing it. When one of the uniformed men glanced up towards the house, Morgan darted back from the glass; he was shocked to realize that, for minutes together, he had forgotten how he looked. Had he been seen by them? he wondered, his heart beating fast. He stood there, trying to calm down. When he heard a noise behind him, he knew that he would find David.

The boy was holding something out to him.

"Don't be afraid," he said, walking towards Morgan. He seemed to have grown in the last few days; not just taller, but older. He looked now like a young adolescent, slightly ungainly, his wrists and ankles too thin for the rest of him. He reminded Morgan of the Doctor, of how the Doctor might have been as a teenage boy, and also of himself; he had Morgan's beauty. Then Morgan saw what he was being offered. He shuddered.

"Where did this come from?" he said.

"That doesn't matter now. Put it on," said the boy in a low flat voice, as though he were talking in his sleep or reading from a card. His eyes were fixed on Morgan's.

Morgan took hold of the hollow face, which felt as though it were made of flesh-coloured wax and weighed almost nothing, and lifted it rapidly to his own. For a moment he could see nothing; he must have closed his eyes as the face approached, its inner side towards him. His hands were brisk and eager as they pressed the cool wax to the wounds and to the part of him that was healthy, without distinction. When he opened his eyes again, both good and bad, he saw that the world was the same and that the eyelids of the face were as able to move as his; *were* his. He parted his lips to speak and the lips of the mask moved with them and the sound they made was the whole sound of a human voice, though unrecognizable to Morgan. Trembling, his hands skirted the edge of the mask, but there was no edge to speak of, only the slightest change in texture as the waxlike skin lapped over and into his own skin, absorbing its warmth. And then even that faint difference seemed to disappear.

"Where did you find this?" Morgan insisted.

David took his hand. "Come downstairs," he said. "We'll see them off."

"The Doctor?" said Morgan, hearing this voice that wasn't his, and yet was.

"Doctor Crane isn't here at the moment," David said. "You'll have to protect us by yourself." He squeezed Morgan's hand in his. "Don't worry. We'll be all right."

Morgan didn't stumble as he walked down the stairs and across the hall. He wasn't sure if it was David's hand that guided him, or his own new eyes, through which he saw the world as two quite separate images for the first few steps and then, with the ease of a hand sliding into the perfect fit of a glove, as one. One world within his eyes: two eyes, one world. He breathed and felt cool air in his mouth and nose, the light and healing flutter of it. By the time he had reached the door, he was aware only of himself. Even David had melted back.

The men were standing in a roughly formed triangle, with Pate at its apex no more than a foot from the door frame. Morgan opened both doors and stepped forward. He smiled and the face smiled with him, but it wasn't *like* that; his whole face smiled, his muscles moving the wax, which no longer felt like wax but was his own flesh. And now this has happened to me, he thought, and I am whole again. And we are here, together, in the house, with our enemy before us. This is too good to miss, it struck him; Engel will surely appear before it is over. He smiled more broadly, raising his good hand to his cheeks to discover dimples. Perhaps I am beautiful again, he thought, the way I used to be before the accident. He wished the house possessed a mirror.

"Yes," he said, and the voice he heard now was the voice he had lost; the hiss had gone. He had forgotten what his voice was like. "Who are you? What do you want?"

"Finally. You must be the owner," said Pate in an officious manner. Trilby, immediately behind his left shoulder, nodded.

"And you are—?"

"From the ministry," said Pate, hostile, aggrieved. "This isn't our first visit."

"So I believe," said Morgan. And then, because the sound of his hissless voice was like music to him, he added, gesturing them into the house, "Please." He knew they would be safe inside, safer even; David would have known what to do.

"You were told, I imagine?"

"Of your previous visit? Yes." Morgan stood to one side as the men entered, bending at the waist to stroke the head of the smaller of the dogs, which allowed this, pulling its head back to lick Morgan's palm with its long dark tongue. The soldier who held the leashes tugged the dog away.

"My mother kept wolfhounds," Morgan said. This was the first dog he had touched since then, he thought, but didn't say.

"We're back here for the children," Pate said. "We know they're being hidden here. You won't get away with it this time."

The tone of the man, both aggressive and base, made

Morgan want to laugh; and so he did. He felt no fear at all, a sensation so new to him he experienced it as power. When he had finished laughing, he said, "There are no children here."

"That's as may be," said Pate. He added, in a tone that struck Morgan as one of pathetic, infantile cunning, "Then you won't have any reason not to allow us to look for them? If there are none?"

"Of course not," Morgan said. He was staring into the house now, towards the rich dark sweep of the stairs. Apart from the snuffling of the dogs at the men's feet, there was absolute silence. He had faith in the children and their ability to disappear when the occasion required it, faith, even more, in David; still, a little more time would hardly hurt. Besides, with his new face, he was curious. "Before you start your futile search, perhaps you could tell me, in the simplest language you know, why the ministry supposes I should be harbouring children? I live here with my housekeeper and a small household of staff I rarely see. I have no wife, no family. My parents are dead. Apart from my dear friend Doctor Crane, whom I believe you have met, I am to all intents and purposes a hermit. What on earth would I do with children? What would children do with me?" How wonderful his voice was, thought Morgan, as clear and crisp as a metal bell. He could have listened to himself all day.

Pate and Trilby glanced at each other.

"Our information is reserved," Pate said.

"And what would you do with any children you found here, assuming you did?" Morgan felt reckless. There was nothing they could do to him, or anyone else. He understood himself as power. The body is a weapon, he thought, in the right hands. He would remember thinking this, much later, when he was telling the Doctor what had happened, and wonder what use he had imagined his body would be when it came to it; he would say it too, and the Doctor would nod, apparently understanding, yet also perhaps perplexed, because Morgan was being anything but clear. In what sense, he would say. The body becomes a weapon most effectively in death, Morgan said, straining forward to be understood.

"There are laws," said Pate.

"With regard to children," said Trilby.

One of the uniformed men coughed and glanced in a helpless sort of way towards the door, now closed. Morgan could see that the man was holding a cigarette, which had burnt down to the tip; there was the scent of burning cork in the hall. Let him sweat a little, he decided, but the black man walked across and opened the door as though the house were his. "I heard a voice," the man said urgently. "There's one outside." Immediately, he was followed by the other men and the dogs, then by Morgan, whose heart was jumping. Was it possible that one of the children had not, somehow, known? Had his faith in their ability been misplaced? He stood on the top step of the flight that led down to the drive and watched as the dogs followed the wall, their noses to the ground, the men behind them in a line. Only Trilby had remained. He was standing beside Morgan as though they had known each other for many years, their coat sleeves almost touching. He had his notebook in one hand, his pencil in the other.

"Your doctor friend isn't here," he said, conversationally.

"And where do you take them, the children you find?

What do you do with them in the end?" Morgan asked again.

"Oh, well, you shouldn't worry about that. Nothing that dreadful happens," Trilby said. They were standing in the drizzle, but Trilby's head was protected. "They're needed, you see." He glanced at Morgan and then at the sky, as if to say he should get himself a hat, and Morgan thought for a moment that his face might be affected by the rain. Then he remembered that wax resisted water and laughed to himself, while Trilby stared after his colleagues. "We couldn't manage without our children. That's all," he said. The group of men and dogs had disappeared behind the corner of the house by now.

"And your task is simply to find them?" Morgan said.

"Yes." Trilby shrugged.

"And are there many lost children?"

Trilby pursed his lips. "More running wild than *lost*. It's for their own good in the end, whatever the number. The weather's getting worse all the time. You'll have noticed? They say the axis of the earth has shifted in the last few decades but I wouldn't know about that. It's not my field, you see. Working in welfare, as I do. I leave that sort of thing to the experts. I find a hat protects me. So much of the body's heat is lost through the head, you know. And, of course, it shelters me against the rain."

That was when they heard one of the dogs begin a furious barking. Trilby headed off to the source of the noise, slowly breaking into a run, while Morgan followed. Above the barking of the dog, to which was added the high-pitched howling of the other beast, Morgan fancied he heard the faint but resilient crying of a child. He thought he recognized the cry as Moira's. His face felt tight on him, as though the wax had shrunk. Surely it couldn't be Moira, he thought. Surely not Moira.

Morgan and Trilby had rounded the corner before they heard the confused shouts of the other men. They were standing in a circle and staring into what might have been a hole, except that there was no hole, there was nothing but the damp grey gravel of the path. Pate turned round and called to Trilby. "Get over here, man, for God's sake. They've taken Mill."

But Morgan was staring at the black man, who had Moira in his arms. The first to arrive in the house, how many years ago now? and yet always a baby, always being carried by one of the others, never alone or in need, as though her well-being were the source of all their well-being, and not only that of the children, but of his and of Engel's. She was lying in the man's arms and her hands were reaching up and touching his face and the glistening locks of his oiled hair, as they had touched Morgan's so often, in a sort of caress; touching them in what seemed to Morgan now the parody of a caress. "No," he cried out as he ran towards the man, but this time the dogs lunged at him with bared teeth, snarling as his mother's dogs might have done, and he backed away. Pate was muttering in a frenzied way to Trilby, who shook his head and looked at the other men. They had moved off into a cluster and were standing at a distance from the house, their boots on the wet grass of the lawn. In front of them, the dogs lay with their front paws stretched out and their tongues lolling from their mouths. The man holding Moira was the only one to seem unperturbed. Morgan felt the water run down his face, and registered this, despite himself, with a shudder of glee, as though nothing had been lost. When Moira turned to him and smiled, he said, "Don't worry." She smiled again. The black man held her up and shook her a little, to make her laugh, but Morgan said, "No, it's cold and raining, you should cover her." He stepped towards the man and held his arms out. "Here," he said, "give her to me now. I'll hold her for you." But Pate stepped forward and took his arm.

"You have some explaining to do," he said. Morgan shook him off.

"I have nothing to explain to you or anyone else," he said.

"One of my men has disappeared," Pate said.

"What has that to do with me?" said Morgan.

"There's no point in your playing the innocent with me. This has to be accounted for."

"Give me my child," said Morgan.

"You have no child," said Trilby, with an air of triumph. "You made that quite clear earlier. You said"—flipping open his notebook to the page— "and I quote: 'I have no wife, no family.'"

"One of my assistants has disappeared in a highly suspicious manner," insisted Pate. "On your property. Which makes you responsible."

"You must be mad," said Morgan. "People don't disappear."

"He was standing beside me one minute," said one of the other men, "and the next thing he was gone. If that's not disappearing, I don't know what is." He shook his head, bemused. "Like bloody magic, it was. There one minute, gone the next."

Moira began to chortle. Morgan looked at her. She was

staring at him, her little fists opening and closing on the air, as though to show him how the trick had been performed. He looked at her, questioningly, and she nodded, as if to say, Yes, aren't I clever. I know exactly what I'm doing. He stepped back with a gesture of submission and she laughed again. When the group of men moved back towards their cars, with the baby girl still in the arms of the man, Morgan stood back and watched them go, afraid only in part that he had misunderstood.

# CHAPTER EIGHTEEN

in which Morgan loses face and considers the substance of air

Doctor Crane didn't come that day, nor the next. He wasn't there when Morgan stood in the hall and called for Engel, and David came down the stairs towards him and said, "Now you must give it back," and Morgan had shaken his head and moaned. He wasn't there when the boy stepped forward and Morgan had lifted his hands to his face to protect himself from this and found that the wax was peeling away from his flesh, both wounded and whole, like snakeskin sloughed, soft in his grasp, a sort of muted silk, which David folded into a tiny square, placing it in the pocket of his shirt. "I wanted Doctor Crane to see me," Morgan said, but David didn't appear to have heard, or, if he had, to have cared. My power has gone, Morgan thought. His good eye rested on the boy's breast pocket. He fought back an urge to tear the mask away, if mask was what it was, to tear it back and let it seal once again to his face. He wanted to be whole again. David must have sensed this. He stepped back, just out of Morgan's reach, shaking his head in a gesture of warning. If only Crane were here, thought Morgan wildly. He'd help me to have what I want. He would understand.

"They've gone," said David.

"They've taken Moira with them," Morgan said, though he recognized as he spoke that there was no need, that

David already knew exactly what had happened outside in the garden. Perhaps he had been watching from a window. "One of the men they brought with them disappeared," Morgan said, and David nodded at this and smiled. Morgan would have asked him what he knew, but, before he had found the words, the boy gave a dismissive shrug with his shoulders. "What can we do about her? How can we get her back? We can't just let her go like this," Morgan said. Daisy had told him to ask David before acting and he had been angry. Now, here he was, asking David for counsel.

"You mustn't worry about Moira," David said. "She'll be all right."

The children swarmed back into the house within half an hour. They ran along the corridors, laughing, throwing themselves into Morgan's arms. They haven't seen me as I really am, he thought, with a trace of bitterness, because that was how he had felt with the face on; as though he were himself again. He wanted to ask for the face a second time, just to show them, but he sensed that David would not allow this. If there had been a mirror in the house, perhaps he would have insisted. Not only for Doctor Crane and the children, but also for himself. He wanted to see himself and find out what he was.

If only Crane had been here, Morgan thought later, and not only to have seen the face, although that was part of Morgan's longing, and regret. With his experience of the world beyond the walls, surely the Doctor would have known what to do. He would have found the words to open the hearts, and arms, of the men and restore Moira to them. But even that wasn't certain. And Crane was softhearted, Morgan knew this, perhaps too softhearted. He might have lost his temper, or worsened the situation in some other way Morgan could only imagine. They had so much to lose, he thought. Sometimes he found himself breathing in the air through his twisted lips as though there were only a certain amount of it, hungrily almost. Thin air, he thought, into thin air. That's what people would say, that Moira has disappeared into thin air. They have come from air and they will return into air. But is that true, he wondered, and what would it mean if it was?

That night, Morgan dreamt that he was choking. At first he thought it was the mask itself that had turned against him, that a plug of the fleshlike wax had somehow formed and was forcing itself deep into his throat. He clawed at his face, in his sleep at first and then, to his horror, in a state of semiwakefulness from which he could not emerge. Writhing in his bed, alive to each sensation, he felt the wax dissolve into something else, some bitter, acrid substance, a burning that was acid, and then not acid, but fire. His lungs were filled with smoke. There was smoke all round him, in a physical space so small he couldn't move, and unbearable, enveloping heat. And he was one of hundreds, thousands, he knew that now. He tried to cry out, but his voice was trapped within his throat as it melted into fat and wax. He lifted his hands to press them against the metal case of his prison, but his hands were dead.

# CHAPTER NINETEEN

in which Mill is discovered and Morgan is not believed

The following day, Engel called Morgan down to say that she had found something in the kitchen. He saw her standing beside the table, with one of the thin metal batons the men had been carrying in her outstretched hand. "I don't know what it is," she said, "but I don't like it. It's not right for this house. It doesn't belong here." He took it from her and weighed it in his palm. He was still shaken from his dream. "It's made of something I've never seen before," he said. There was a button set into the part shaped for the hand. He touched it and felt a shock shoot up his arm as the baton jumped and sparked. "You see," said Engel. "What did I tell you?" When one of the little boys ran in with a scrap of cloth in his hand, Morgan asked to see it. It was brown, with buttons along one edge. He recognized it as a piece of the missing man's shirt. "Where did you find this?" he said. "Outside," said the boy, whose name was Martin, "in the garden." "Show me," said Morgan, and Martin led him out of the house and along the path that ran towards the boathouse. Halfway down the path, he stopped and pointed into a bush. "In there," he said. Morgan crouched down to see what else there might be, but the inside of the bush was dark and empty of everything but its own thorny tangle of branches. If only Crane were here to help me decide what to do, thought Morgan; something dreadful is happening to us all and I am lost and I have lost my face. "Is this all you found?" he said. "Oh no," said Martin. "Where is the rest of it?" Morgan asked and Martin ran off once more, with Morgan behind him, back to the house.

Upstairs, in the room where the woman made of wax was closed inside her wooden trunk, he found some of the other children. They were sitting in a circle and in the middle of the circle was a tidy heap of fragments of what looked like cloth and leather, buttons, shards of white, some sort of cushion stuffing. The children were laughing and playing with these fragments; they seemed unaware of his presence. One of the babies lifted a scrap of something soft and pink to suck. Morgan walked over and looked more closely and then stepped back, his hand over his mouth.


"They were pieces of skin, I'm sure of it, pieces of skin and bone. And there was hair as well, hanks of hair with the scalp still attached. It looked as though the poor man had been put through a shredding machine. It was awful, Crane, awful," Morgan said, his voice breaking, "and the worst thing was the way they were playing with it, as though it had no value."

"They're only children," said the Doctor, though he didn't mean this. He was as horrified as Morgan. But something had to be said and he didn't know what else would do. And it was true, at least, that they were children. Surely they couldn't have known what they were doing.

"It's not just that they were playing with it, though God knows that was bad enough," said Morgan, shaking his head with horror. "It's the *fun* they were having. Because they knew what it was, you see. I could tell they did." His one good eye stared at Crane, who turned away, abashed, not wanting to be seen as a fool, or naive, but still refusing to accept what Morgan was saying. "They knew what it was, and they were glad. They were having their revenge."

"And your face?" Crane said, in a low voice.

"My what? Oh, that. It was like being born again," Morgan said, with a scoffing laugh. So David must have told him, he thought. There would be no secrets. "I wish you could have seen. I was myself with it on, or thought I was. I can't explain it." He shook his head again, less with horror now than disbelief. "After David made me take it off, I hated him. I wanted the thing back at once, I felt incomplete. But I was wrong to want it like that, I see that now. Because I wasn't myself when I was wearing it, not really. I was stronger than I am without it, not just because I was no longer afraid to be seen, but because I felt superior to the others. And that's not a good strength, is it? I felt like a god." He shuddered. "It scared me, Crane, that sense that everything I did was justified, not by any external law, but because there was no law. I was the law. I would have killed them myself if I'd had the chance. I wouldn't have thought twice, I'm sure of it. Killed them and been glad they were dead. But I didn't have the chance, or I didn't notice it if I had, because there was something of me there that stopped it, I suppose, something of what I am." He paused, then touched his face. "Of what this has made me." He wanted some word of comfort from Crane, but the Doctor didn't speak.

"Then, when I saw what had really happened, when I went upstairs and saw the children treating a dead man like a broken toy, I knew that I *had* done it after all, though I still don't know how, I still don't understand the connection. All I know is that if I hadn't worn that face nothing would have happened. They would just have gone away, I'm sure of it. And David knows that too. Which makes us both responsible."

Crane was at a loss. He wasn't sure he believed Morgan, that was the problem. How could a face made of wax, which must surely have been taken from the head that David had found in the attic, become attached to Morgan's face, and work, and move? It was natural that Morgan should imagine something like this, the poor man; he had all the reason in the world for allowing such a tragic fantasy to take hold of him, to be whole and proud; to be like a god, as he had just said. To want something that badly; no wonder he had let himself be convinced. Yet he *had* opened the door to the men, he *had* been there when Moira was taken away, in full view of them all; these were things that Morgan would never have done if he had been forced to be seen as he was, disfigured. So what other explanation could there be but Morgan's? The Doctor had spoken to David about the face, a few brief words in the hall, but David had been evasive and then obstinate, refusing to say whether Morgan's story was true, although he would surely have known. It was the boy's doing, after all, if it were true. Crane had gone up to the attic and had found the head as he had last seen it, with the face securely hinged. He touched it, hesitant, feeling idiotic, to see if it was warm; it had the warmth of wax but nothing more than that; it had nothing human. He had looked into its eyes to see what could be seen, but all they did was reflect his own.

Morgan didn't need to speak to David about what he

had seen. It was clear that David knew. Perhaps Engel, who had silently gathered the remains of the man into a sack and carried them into the garden to be burnt, had spoken to him; perhaps she had also known. There was no astonishment in the house, thought Morgan, with a shock of understanding; that was the worst thing. No one but he was startled or disconcerted by anything that happened, the coming and the going, the horror, because that was the only word for it, of the man's reappearance.

And then there was Moira. What on earth shall we do about Moira? Morgan thought. David had told him not to worry with such a confident air that he had felt himself calmed, as though from now on the boy would always know better than he, or anyone else, would. But the Doctor was less convinced.

"We can't just let her go like this. I'll see what can be done," he insisted. "It's kidnapping, after all, unless they leave a document of some sort. A receipt, I suppose you'd have to call it." He gave a humourless laugh. "She might be your daughter for all they know, even if you did say you'd never had children. You could have been lying. That wouldn't have been so strange after all. People lie under stress. Under torture. You were hardly obliged to tell them the truth, were you?" But Morgan shrugged in a hopeless way, as though his only decision was to wait for David to tell him what next to do.

After the men and dogs had taken Moira away, Morgan, David, and the Doctor began to spend more time together, walking around the garden or sitting in the Doctor's room, although none of them did more than pretend to work, or read, sometimes with the older ones among the children, more often not. Morgan felt all three of them were waiting for something. Then, late one morning, David said that the car was ready.

"I saw Mr. Green after breakfast," he said. "He says we shall need some more petrol if we are to go very far, but that everything is in perfect working order." David grinned. "It's a beauty, Morgan, it really is," he said, because he had started to use Morgan's name like this, as though they were equals, the way the Doctor did. "He took me for a drive in it. Not far, just out of the garage and back in again, really, but it makes no noise at all. Inside, you feel like you're in a great big boat. He let me drive it a little too. It was easy. I never knew. Mr. Green said I was a natural driver." David's cheeks were flushed with pleasure. He looked exactly like a normal boy, thought Morgan, like any other boy of his age who has been behind the wheel of a car and felt its power succumb to his. Perhaps I am wrong to wonder about them; to wonder and to worry. Perhaps I am the strange one after all. He smiled and nodded.

"We can go and see the car this afternoon," he said, turning to Crane. "Take it out, perhaps. Would you like that? You were keen on the idea, I seem to remember. You thought we could use it, I'm not sure why."

Crane jumped up from the desk, as thrilled as the boy. "Your father's car?" he said. "The one he was driving when he died?"

"Yes," said Morgan, "though it's more like a tank than a car. A rich man's tank. White leather upholstery, if my memory serves me. And my grandfather's coat of arms on the door."

"Yes," said David, more excited than before, fired by

the Doctor, "and wood, it's lined with wood inside. You can smell the polish."

"I can get petrol," Crane said. "I have an allowance, as a doctor. It isn't much but it'll get us into town and back."

"Into town?" said Morgan.

"Or anywhere else," the Doctor said rapidly, as if to take back his words. "Though town is the safest place these days, oddly enough. It's not like the country, you know. Not anymore. In the country anything can happen."

"Yet it never does," said Morgan. "Not here at least."

"That's because you protect us here," said David, reaching out to squeeze Morgan's wounded hand in an odd, adult way. "You keep us safe."

"I always thought it was you, David, you and the others, who protected me," said Morgan wryly, wanting to withdraw his hand yet, more deeply, anxiously happy to have it held. "I certainly didn't keep Moira safe."

"Moira didn't need to go," said David.

"What do you mean?" said Morgan.

"Not if it hadn't been needed in another way, I mean."

"Another way?" said the Doctor.

David nodded. "You'll see. Don't worry." He turned to Melissa, who had walked into the room while he was speaking. He must have heard her steps. She was just inside the door, ignoring the two men, her eyes on David. "Won't they, Melissa? They'll all see. We'll show them."

"The car's ready then?" she said to David. He nodded. "Yes," he said. "It's nearly time to go."

She grinned. "I'll tell the others."

# CHAPTER TWENTY

in which the children sing

Later that day Morgan went upstairs, to the room where the woman was kept, and found that she had been removed from the box. She had been placed upright in the centre of the room, on a carved wooden stand that raised her to what would have been her normal height. Around her, kneeling or seated, were the children, all of the children as far as Morgan could tell. He stood by the door, all at once unnerved, afraid to be seen; the room was so full of children, circle upon concentric circle, with the calmly smiling woman of wax and paint at the heart of it. For a moment his mind went back to that other circle of children, these same children, around what was left of the man. He shuddered, closed his eyes against the unwanted image.

The door to her womb had been closed and she was perfect; she might have been alive. For a moment, Morgan thought he saw her move, the pale extended hand turned up a little as if to beckon him across to her, her mouth trembling faintly as if she were about to speak. But he couldn't be sure. He was about to turn and leave, still shaken, not wanting to be there, when he became aware of a noise in the room, so low as to be almost imperceptible; a sort of crooning composed of many tiny threads of sound. He listened harder. It was the children. The children were singing. He knew that he had been seen and that his presence didn't matter. He was neither welcome nor unwelcome. The children were shoulder to shoulder, rocking from left to right as they sang, their movement as slight, unearthly, as their song. Where are they from? he thought, for the thousandth time. Who are they? What do they want from me? And then, as sounds become clearer the longer you listen, he heard what the song was saying. It was the first syllable of human speech to be uttered in almost every part of the world, he had read this in a book of his grandfather's about language. Ma-ma-ma-ma. The primal sound, a simple parting of the lips around air, that makes us what we are.

# CHAPTER TWENTY-ONE

in which the car is tested for the first time
and David is curious

The first time, Crane took the wheel. They followed the drive to the gate, Morgan and David beside the Doctor, with half a dozen of the children crowded into the backseat of the car. David was right; the car was almost silent. With all the windows closed, Morgan had the sense of being in an aquarium. There was something about the window glass, its thickness probably, that gave the sense of water, though whether the water was inside or outside the glass was impossible to tell. Morgan felt that he was breathing a substance that was heavier and more viscous than air.

The car glided slowly along the drive until they were within feet of the gate, which stood open as it always did, because the knowledge of the monster inside the house was enough, supposed Morgan, to protect it from intruders. Then Crane stopped and glanced across David at Morgan, who shook his head. A moan of disappointment rose from the backseat, but David turned round swiftly and hushed them. "He's right. Not yet," he said. "We're still not ready."

"Ready for what?" said Morgan.

David was normally so patient. But this time he said, "How many times must you ask and not be told before you stop? Why can't you just wait?"

"You have no right, David, to talk to me in this manner," said Morgan, irritated, but also unnerved, as though a trusted, favourite dog had growled at his touch.

"I have no right?" said David, in a voice and tone that Morgan had never heard before, both authoritative and hurt. "*You* have no right to question me."

"That's quite enough," said Crane. "David, behave yourself. How dare you talk to Morgan like that? After all he has done for you. For all of you."

"You're right," said David, flushed with anger. "I'm sorry," he muttered, but not to Morgan, his head cast down. One of the smaller children giggled and Morgan's horrified instinct was to reach round and slap her, because he was afraid to slap David, who was quivering with rage beside him. It would have been like striking the dog, the dog he thought he knew. Cautiously, he touched the boy's shoulder.

"We needn't argue, you know," he said, his voice breaking with emotion. "If you would only tell me your purpose, David, share it with me. I know you have one, and I know that I am part of it, we all are, which makes it worse, my curiosity I mean. I wonder what use I can possibly be to you, you see." He paused. "The truth is that I'm scared. I don't want to let you down."

"You won't," whispered David. "Just trust me. Just do what I say. Then everything will be all right. You won't let us down."

"We won't let you," said Melissa from behind.

"The next time," said Crane, "I'll bring some petrol with me. It won't be difficult."

"What?" said Morgan. "On your bicycle?"

Crane laughed. "No," he said as he turned the car and drove it back towards the garage. "I do still have my car, you know, though I rarely use it unless I have to. For house calls, occasionally. Nothing like this, of course. I've never needed an armoured limousine with its own coat of arms. Your father must have been very rich."

"He was," said Morgan. "And so am I, thanks to him. And to my grandfather, of course."

"It was your grandfather who made all the money though, wasn't it?" said David. "Your father just made sure that it wasn't frittered away. He just held on to it."

Morgan was startled. "What on earth do you know about my grandfather?"

David looked at him, apparently just as surprised. "But everything in this house was your grandfather's once, wasn't it? It was all his stuff, the furniture, the books, the carpets, the woman. The boathouse. Even though he never saw it, not even once. We'd none of us be here, none of us, if it wasn't for him."

"But he's been dead for years," said Morgan.

"I know that," said David. "But I've been reading about him. I found his diary, I suppose it was, and it's all about what he did before he had this house built, when he was travelling around all those different countries. He thought he was a good man, your grandfather."

"My mother didn't think he was," Morgan said. "He just took what he wanted from wherever he found it, she always said."

"That doesn't matter," said David firmly. "She doesn't count."

"Your mother's dead," said Melissa, with an air of such satisfaction that Morgan wondered, with a sense of chill, if she had ever had any notion of what it meant to have a mother. Yet he had seen her cling to Engel, and cry to be picked up. He had seen her run towards him as he walked across the garden, and raise her face to his, unflinching, to be kissed.

# CHAPTER TWENTY-TWO

in which Morgan and David visit the boathouse

A few days later David brought the wax face back to Morgan and told him that it was time they went to look for Moira. Morgan shook his head nervously. "I don't want to," he said, his voice sounding strange to him. "That makes no difference," David said. "It's time to go. If we don't go now, we'll miss our chance." He held the face out. "Come on," he said, and it was as if he had understood that Morgan really wanted to put the face on again; despite himself he gave a slow knowing smile, his hands quite steady. Morgan took the face, as loose and fine as silk, softer than he remembered it, more skinlike, and raised it towards his eyes and it seemed to move of its own accord until it was sealed to his skull as closely as if it had been his own face, so that he felt, his heart beating rapidly, that it was. He was whole again. He strode around the mirrorless house, followed by David, who eventually said that he could see himself in the water if he wanted. They went down to the boathouse together.

"This is where it happened," said David, when they were both in the boathouse, standing side by side at the edge of the water. It was cooler and darker than in the garden, the tongue of lake a still, dark glass by their feet. Morgan leant forward a little, remained transfixed. David said again, in the same measured tone, "This is where it happened." Morgan came to himself and stepped back.

"Yes," he said.

"And this is where it will end," said David.

Morgan was startled. "Where what will end?" He waited for an answer, but David was silent. He knelt beside Morgan's feet and trailed his adolescent hand in the still water, backwards and forwards, until Morgan's face was fractured into ribbons, lifting and falling. He caught a scent of blood in the air.

"I should like to go out in a boat," said David.

Morgan shook his head.

"Why not?"

Morgan shook his head a second time, but did not speak.

"We may need to use the boat to find Moira."

"Don't be silly, David."

This time, it was David's turn to shake his head. "You have no idea where she is, do you? She may be at sea. We have to be prepared."

It took Morgan a moment to realize that David, serious David, was teasing him. He leant forward again and there he was, his perfection, the dreadful lie of it, on his face for all to see, except that only those who knew him would know that it was a lie. So perhaps it wasn't a lie at all, he told himself. This is the face I would have had, he thought; it belongs to me.

"My father took me out in a boat once," David said, "when I was very young. We went fishing on a lake like this, but larger. There were tall trees all round, they made the water dark. It was a rowing boat and we tried to row together, but I was too small and we kept going round in circles. My father took over in the end. We stopped at the other side of the lake, in the shadow of the trees, and my father showed me how to bait my line. It was very quiet there, if I hadn't been with my father I would have been afraid. After we'd been there I don't know how long, waiting for a fish to bite, my father said that he'd caught something. He had to stand up it was so big. He had to fight to bring it towards the boat. I thought he was going to overturn the boat and I wanted to make him stop, but I was too scared to stand up in case I made it worse. He reeled his line in with the rod bending—it took forever—until I thought it would break and then, there it was, a long grey fish in the bottom of the boat, grey and green, bright and hard, with a yellow belly, and so angry. I've never seen anything so angry. It twisted and flapped and all I wanted to do was save it. I think my father knew that because he unhooked the fish, then picked it up in both his arms and threw it back into the lake."

"You've never told me about your father," said Morgan, but what he thought was, So David has a father, after all. "Where is he now? Do you know?"

"That's all there is to tell," said David. He looked up at Morgan, who remembered that he was wearing the face of wax. He was ashamed for a moment, and lifted his hand as if to take it off, but David smiled at him and stopped the hand with his own. "That's when they came for him, you see, for all of us. That was the last day I saw him. We heard them from the boat. The shouting, people running. There were shots. He thought we'd be safer on land. I was taken away and left somewhere safe. That's what they thought, anyway."

"Where are you from?" said Morgan. He heard pain in his voice, and fear of what David might say, as though there could be no good answer to his question.

"I'm from where we were taken," said David. "We all are." And then he turned away, and would say no more. They left the boathouse. It had started to rain and the grass was cushion-soft and wet beneath their feet. When Morgan asked him about Moira, and what David had meant when he had brought him the face and said they would search for her, the boy turned on Morgan in a kind of fury.

"I don't know everything," he said. "Can't you understand that? It isn't my fault. Why can't you all leave me alone?"

# CHAPTER TWENTY-THREE

*in which they take the car beyond the wall*

One day, not long after this, they decided they would take the car outside the grounds. Morgan drove, with the Doctor beside him to make sure that he knew what to do. He had driven years before, not only this car but a smaller one of his mother's, although they had never gone more than a few miles before she insisted on being taken home; she would sit in the backseat as though Morgan were her driver, swathed in scented Indian shawls, muttering to herself with a suffering air, then tap his shoulder to say that her dogs would be missing her, they would have to return at once.

There were four of the children in the back. David, of course, with Daisy, a toddler in her arms, and Melissa. Morgan had called the toddler August because that was the month he had been found, but the other children called him Mite, and that was the only name he recognized. He was fast asleep and seemed to be dreaming. "Wouldn't it be better to leave him at home?" Morgan had said as they approached the gate, but David shook his head. "No, no," he said. "We might need him later." "Might need him? What do you mean?" But David stared out through the window and didn't answer. A few moments later, he pointed to a tree at the side of the road as Morgan drove slowly past. "That's a willow, isn't it?" The Doctor nodded. "I see you've been studying trees," he said. "Oh yes, I need to know about everything, just in case," said David in his solemn way. Then, in a quieter voice, he added: "Aren't you afraid of being seen?" And Morgan turned and nodded, because he had been waiting for this; had hoped to provoke it. "Then you'd better have this," David said and gave him the face. With Crane's hand steadying the wheel as the car moved forward, Morgan lifted the face to his own face and felt it seal to the warmth of his furrowed skin, as though it knew what to do without his bidding. Morgan had seen what he looked like, in the still dark water inside the boathouse, but he couldn't resist the temptation to turn the mirror in the car towards him and take a second look. How strange it was, he thought, to see himself like this. Yet no one else seemed to find it strange. Even Crane, who had never seen the face on his before, seemed calmly to accept it. He was staring ahead, his hand still on the steering wheel, but Morgan had caught him glance across and nod, already used, it seemed, to the idea. How quickly we learn, thought Morgan. That was all it took to get used to the idea. Everything became inevitable with time.

It took no more than an hour to reach the outskirts of the city, driving directly west towards the risen sun. Morgan had expected interruptions, disturbance, he wasn't sure of what kind, but the roads had been almost empty. He was, perversely, disappointed. A dozen or so men, most dressed in mismatched pieces of uniform, turned to watch the car and its occupants from the overgrown verges, halting until the car had passed, their faces wary, their hands gripped tight round whatever they had to hold. Morgan's first instinct was to flinch, but there was no need for that. He felt an unaccustomed warmth in his cheeks, almost a stinging, as though they had been rubbed with alcohol. He stared back at the men as he drove past. He found himself wishing, despite his better instinct, that they could know what he really looked like, wanting to dare them to see what that might be. "Where are the walls?" he said at one point, as the car rose up a low hill and they saw the countryside around, barren and with burnt-out houses dotted across it. "There's nothing left to protect round here," said Crane. "It's all been destroyed, by fire and time and neglect, if nothing else. That's why we're left alone at the house, I suppose. Most people have forgotten we're there."

"I thought it was I that scared them off," said Morgan, with a laugh, feeling his warm cheeks taut on the bone.

"Well, yes, that too, I imagine," murmured Crane. "They're fools enough for that."

They came to a stop at a red-and-white-striped metal bar that had been lowered across the road. A man approached them from a wooden hut at the far side of the bar. The children in the backseat began to wriggle with excitement as Morgan wound down the window to greet him. Bending, the man stared into the car, then nodded.

"Good morning, Doctor," he said. For a moment Morgan thought that the man was talking to him, but before he could speak the Doctor had already leant across to answer. The man was standing back by this time to look at the car. He bent down once again to see inside. He hadn't shaved; his uniform was creased and soiled along the collar.

"Nice car," he said.

"It's mine," said Morgan, who wanted to feel once more the effect on the skin of speaking.

"I haven't seen one like this for a few years," the soldier said, stepping back. He stood where he was, looking around as though he had heard a noise, then walked to the end of the bar and raised it. As soon as the bar was vertical, he waved them through, his hands on his hips, his feet apart. They were almost beyond the barrier when the soldier lifted an arm to stop them and called something out. Morgan almost continued to drive; if Crane hadn't touched his thigh with a warning hand he would have.

"I suppose you've got business in town," the soldier said to Morgan.

"Yes," said Morgan, feeling the smile in his perfect new face, enjoying the tension of muscle and sinew. "Ministry business."

"Only I ought to see official papers of some kind, you see," said the soldier, as though the words were being dictated to him by someone else. He looked behind Morgan, then back into Morgan's eyes. "Seeing that it's the Doctor, though, I don't suppose it matters."

Morgan turned round to look at David, who shrugged. The Doctor laughed, then leant across Morgan to speak directly to the soldier.

"How's the back?" he said. "I do hope the irritation's eased." The soldier blushed.

"I do have papers, if necessary," Morgan said, but the soldier had moved away from the car, apparently embarrassed.

"No, no," he said, waving them on. "There's no need for that."

The road beyond the metal bar was identical, with its

ragged unkempt verges and vista of grey fields. Soon, though, houses began, at first one or two, often unoccupied, and then in groups of half a dozen or more, with rusted bicycles propped outside and dirty curtains at the windows. Sometimes a curtain would twitch and then fall back into place.

"It wasn't his back that needed treatment," the Doctor said, with a laugh, as a child ran out from one of the houses, almost in front of the car, then pulled up sharply. Morgan swerved and would have continued, but David told him to stop, and Morgan instantly obeyed. David opened the back door of the car and beckoned the child across. It was a boy, a little younger than David, in a worn grey suit that was far too big for him; the jacket sleeves had been rolled up, the trousers cut down to fit and hitched in with string. He had no shirt under the jacket, just bare white skin. He was thin, with pale tangled hair that fell to his shoulders, which made him look less feminine than wild. He stared at David, his mouth falling open.

"What do you want?" he said.

"What do *you* want?" David replied. He moved over on the backseat, to make room. "Come with us." The boy looked mortified and turned his head away.

"I can't."

"You can if you want," said David, his voice almost indifferent. "They won't miss you."

The boy grinned then, as if he had found a friend, and climbed into the car beside David. "They will be glad," he said, when Morgan turned to examine him more closely. "He's right." He grinned again, at Morgan this time. "I was going to leave anyway, one of these days. Any day now."

"We seem to have another charge," the Doctor said quietly. He reached between his legs to a basket he had brought, and pulled out a tin of biscuits Engel had packed for them and a flask of milky tea. The boy reached forward hungrily then paused, as if some notion of politeness had occurred to him. But the Doctor opened the tin and offered the biscuits to them all. "You'll have to drink out of the flask, one after the other," he said. "I don't have enough cups."

"He can have mine," said Morgan. Through the rearview mirror he watched the boy drink greedily from his cup, grab biscuits, cram them into his mouth, swallow them almost whole, his white throat working. Morgan hadn't imagined this, such hunger. He was shocked; his understanding of the outside world had been so tame, so feeble. As they continued along the barely surfaced road towards what must be the centre of the city and the houses became larger, although always run-down and often derelict, he thought about his father, who had driven this same car along these same roads, and who must have seen all this a thousand times. What had he thought about as he drove, or was driven by others? His own house, with its walls and lake, its rooms filled with furniture and porcelain and carpets from countries he had never seen and the distant soothing rustle of people at work to keep him in this comfort? His wife and her exquisite clothes and shoes, which came from other cities than this, larger more splendid cities, famous cities whose names were poetry, and which seemed to speak only of taste? Had he thought about his son, the beautiful child who would one day inherit everything, the wealth that he had also inherited, but also conserved, and encouraged to grow? Had he felt shame, ever, for more than a moment, like a breeze from a window briefly opened and then closed again for good? And Morgan thought about his mother and her contempt, which had reached so far and so deep within her it had left no room for anything else, and had then reached out and burnt him, as certainly as the acid had done.

The boy wiped his mouth on his sleeve and looked around him at the other children. He held out his hand to David in the oddly formal way so many of the children seemed to have, thought Morgan, as though it were not a formality at all but natural to them, and said that his name was Godfrey but that everyone called him Goddie for short. "It sounds like Goodie," said Melissa, and he grinned. "That's what my little brother calls me," he said, "only he can't say the g, he just says *oodie*." He reached out then and lifted Mite away from Daisy and held him up, making the child giggle. "Godfrey's a dreadful name," said Daisy. It was the first time she had spoken since the car had left the grounds of the house. Now she pressed her face against the glass and began to sing a song that Morgan didn't recognize, too low for him initially to catch the words. Straining his ears, he heard a word or two, a phrase, a snatch of phrases, until it became clear to him, with a shiver of delight, that she was singing what she saw. Cars and trees and gardens and a woman with red hair and bicycles and soldiers and a dog with three legs and a dead thing that looks like a cat and two flowers on a branch and heaps of rubbish, all in a singsong tone as though she were reciting a mantra, and a man with a spade and a telephone box and a blue car and a brown car. After a minute or two, Melissa joined in, in perfect unison. How odd that she knows what to notice, thought Morgan, despite his awareness that he ought to be used to this sort of thing by now, this synchronicity of thought and deed among the children. He shouldn't be surprised if David and Mite joined in as well; even Goddie, who was sitting in the middle of the children with an ecstatic smile, Mite on his lap. He would also know what to see and do.

"Here we are," said Crane in an urgent tone some moments later, when Morgan had simply been driving along the road, not looking at what passed so much as listening to the song of it.

"Here, where?" he said.

"We have to turn down here," said Crane, gesturing across Morgan towards a turning on the left. "That's where the ministry is."

"No," said David. "Moira isn't at the ministry."

"Where is she?" Crane said.

"Keep driving. I'll tell you when to turn."

Morgan drove for another half mile, waiting for David to tell him what he should do. Goddie was becoming agitated, twisting around in the seat to stare at the road behind them; but Morgan, through the rearview mirror, saw David whisper in his ear. "No, no, you don't understand, you don't know them like I do," said Goddie. "If we go too close, they'll get us." He pulled as David took his hand and held it tight, but couldn't break away. "David knows best," said Melissa. "You have to trust him, like the rest of us do." She craned forward and touched Morgan's neck gently with her fingers, which were cool and soft, Morgan noticed; he could feel them through what? his skin or the skin of the thing he was wearing? But what was his skin and what wasn't? Where was the edge? "You're much prettier like this, Morgan," she said, with a little laugh, "but I like you better as you really are. When you're you."

David told him to stop for a moment. Morgan pulled over and turned to look at the children, who were sitting there in a row in the back of the car, their faces slightly raised as if to sniff the air, like mice aroused by a distant whiff of cheese, thought Morgan. Then David smiled and nodded. "All right," he said, "you have to drive on until you see a big grey stone place with a sort of tower on the right and coloured glass in the windows, and then you go right and right again. I'll tell you when to stop."

"That's a church," said Morgan.

"What?"

"The big place you described. It's called a church."

"And that's where you go right," repeated David, with a trace of impatience in his voice, as though what things were called no longer mattered.

Morgan did as he was told.

"But where are we going?" he said, after turning right twice as David had directed him. They were on a wide road, recently resurfaced, with two lanes on each side divided by a low concrete wall, making it impossible to turn except at certain points where the wall was interrupted. There was no other traffic. On the far side of the road was an area of grass, hundreds of yards deep, with ribbons of concrete crisscrossing it. Morgan assumed it was an airport, although he hadn't seen one for fifteen years, maybe more. He had waved his father off on a journey once, as a boy; he remembered watching from the roof of a large glass building as the nose of the plane lifted up, so sharply it took his breath away. His mother was with him, she held

his hand and then his shoulder and then her hand fell away
and the plane was so far off he could barely see it and then
it had disappeared and he had thought, maybe my father
will never come back, and there will be just the two of us.
Already Rebecca had fallen away. Perhaps it was here, he
thought, perhaps this was the airport. He glanced across as
he drove. Low metal structures with curved roofs could be
seen in the distance, blurred by a fine low mist that had
begun to drift across the empty field towards them. There
were no planes, only trucks and platforms of various kinds
on wheels. Perhaps it was not an airport at all, but something
else. Perhaps from above, the ribbons would form a pattern
of some kind, thought Morgan, would form a sign. And
someone would read it and understand.

On their side of the road, set back about fifty yards from
the metal railings, was a low sprawling building that seemed
to go on forever. It must have been extended many times,
its style changed every fifty yards or so, as did the materials
that had been used to construct it, stone, brick, concrete;
the windows were large or small or simply absent, the roof
changed colour, dipped and then rose. The walls of the
building had been painted white, each section at different
times, there was a sort of pulse of grey as the colour faded
away and was renewed, although some sections were better
maintained than others. Behind the building chimneys
rose in groups of two and three, working chimneys with
smoke pouring from them; it must be a factory of some sort,
thought Morgan. The railings were interrupted by tall iron
gates every twenty or thirty yards. These had been opened
and people were streaming towards them in groups, or twos
and threes; they didn't look towards the car, not even when

David told Morgan to drive more slowly now because they would soon be turning off the road, they were almost there. It had started to rain and Morgan turned on the windscreen wipers, which made two perfect arcs in front of his eyes. He could smell the fear coming off the new boy, what was his name? He glanced towards the mirror and saw the child's wild eyes, framed by his hair, as long and fine as a girl's. Goddie. His own heart was pumping as he drove, with the factory stretched out beside him like a sleeping beast. So this was where he would find Moira, the first child of them all, he told himself.

He wasn't surprised when David told him to turn in through the largest of the gates; he wasn't surprised when his eye was caught by the high arch over the gate, which bore, entwined in flowers and leaves of gilded iron, the name of the factory; he wasn't surprised when he saw that the name at the centre of the arch was his, his family name. Fletcher. Maker of arrows. The coat of arms above the name was the one his grandfather had designed from his summerhouse in Ecbatana, the coat of arms his mother had despised so much. He had finally been brought home, if home was the source of it all, of his wealth at least. I've never been here, he thought, and was about to say this to the Doctor, who might not even have noticed the significance of where they were, but a small hand on his shoulder warned him.

"You're someone else now," David said. "Not really, of course, *we* know that. We know you're Morgan. But you mustn't think of yourself, do you see? You must think only of Moira, because you don't matter. None of us do right now, all right? Drive through and when they try to stop you, tell them you're bringing them some new children. They'll understand. If they say we can't go in, it doesn't matter. Don't argue, all right? Just turn round and drive out again. We've got other ways."

The Doctor produced an odd noise in his throat, half laugh, half cough. "It's all in David's hands, apparently," he said to no one in particular, so that everyone would hear, and when Morgan thought of how control had been usurped by David, it was with a sense of relief, as something inevitable. "All right," he said. Goddie whimpered in the back, crouched down between the girls, his hands held up to his face. Daisy put her arm across his head, as if to both protect and conceal him. "Don't worry," Melissa said in a sharper voice than usual. "Nothing's going to happen to us. I mean, this whole place belongs to Morgan. We're perfectly safe here."

"Shut up," snapped David.

"Well, it does," said Melissa. "You can't tell us everything all the time. You can't tell us all what to do every time. We aren't fools, David. You aren't God."

Morgan halted the car outside what appeared to be the central section of the building. In front of his eyes, a flight of grey marble steps led to a series of glass and metal doors, through which nothing could be seen. Two armed men in black capes stood at each door. Morgan touched his face with hesitant fingers. He moved his features tentatively, a smile, a frown, until David nudged his shoulder from behind. "It's all right," he said. "Let's go."

# CHAPTER TWENTY-FOUR

in which Morgan and the children enter the factory

The Doctor got out of the car first and opened a large umbrella for the children. Goddie refused to leave his seat, but the other three jumped down with excitement, David with Mite in his arms. Melissa turned to Goddie, but Daisy hurriedly pulled her away, whispering something in her ear, and Melissa shrugged and left the car. David hurried towards her, holding Mite out for her to take. "You can look after him," he said. Morgan watched them as they walked towards the steps, which were dark and gleaming with the rain, then joined them, playing with the car keys in a nervous way, but refusing to stand beneath the umbrella, enjoying the touch of the water on his face, which felt both protected and exposed. He raised his eyes and saw the sopping flags along the top of the building. How powerful we must be, he thought, we operate all over the world. Perhaps the airport is ours as well. Turning his head each way, behind him and farther on, he could see no end to the factory as it stretched into the distance; it seemed to curve with the earth. It occurred to him then that he had no concrete notion what might be produced in this building, which fed and clothed him now as it had when he was a child, as it had his mother. His father had said they sold their goods overseas, that was why he travelled so much, so far, the hundreds of beautiful objects in the house that his grandfather had gathered from all over the world were often gifts from grateful customers. But what had his grandfather's actual business been? At the end of his life he had been obsessed by knowledge, finally by medicine, that was clear from his library, from the presence of the anatomical figures, he had devoted all his time to it. But before that? Arms, he had supposed, but this supposition had had no consequence until now. Perhaps he had been obsessed by power all the time, it occurred to Morgan; power over what people knew, and what they were, the way their bodies worked. The way their bodies could be destroyed.

They had reached the top of the steps when one of the uniformed men stepped forward, holding his rifle across his chest. Morgan saw that the badge on his cap bore the family's coat of arms. These men belong to me, he thought, and it occurred to him that they would know nothing of his accident. They might have heard rumours, for surely people would have talked about his absence, there must have been stories of the recluse in the country house, of the madwoman and her dogs; but whatever they had heard, no guard would dare deny him access to his own factory. This made him smile. When the man held his rifle out to bar the door, Morgan rested his hand on it and the man was startled. Then he remembered what David had said he must do. Very well, he would try that first.

"We have some children for you," he said. The man shrugged, his face impassive once again. This didn't surprise Morgan. He wondered what effect his words were supposed to have. What sense would children have in a place like this? What purpose would they serve? He glanced down at David beside him, who was staring at the man and frowning, his face in the shade of the Doctor's umbrella. Mite had begun to whimper and struggle in Melissa's arms; she was clutching him as though scared he might run off, although he could barely walk. Despite the Doctor's umbrella, they were all getting wet. Morgan was about to turn away when the oldest among the armed men walked across.

"Where did you find that car?" he said, pointing his rifle at the forecourt behind them. Morgan's eyes followed the gesture, noticing once again the coat of arms on the driver's-side door, then turned his gaze towards the man, who stared at him, with initial hesitation and then a sort of startled shame, before lowering his eyes and stepping back.

"Master Morgan?" he said, his voice breaking. "I'm sorry, sir, I didn't see who you were at first. It's been so long."

"Too long," said Morgan, thrilled. He had been recognized. David strained up to whisper. "Say you want to see your sister." Morgan nodded.

"I'll have the car parked for you, sir," the man said.

"There's no need for that," said Morgan. "We shall be needing it again soon enough." He looked at the Doctor. "Perhaps we should be getting on with our business."

"Quite," said the Doctor, nodding his head, although it was evident, to Morgan at least, that Crane had not the slightest idea of how to proceed. But the guard had brushed aside the younger man and opened the door.

"Come in, sir, out of the rain. All of you. The children will be drenched."

The Doctor shook and closed the umbrella as the children followed Morgan into the building. They found themselves in a large, bare atrium, as vast as a church, at the far side of which was a series of gleaming metal desks and, behind each desk, a woman. Each woman also wore a uniform, Morgan noticed as he walked across the gleaming floor with the children and the Doctor behind him; light grey jacket and white blouse with a small black bow at the neck. They looked like schoolmistresses. This would have been his sister's doing, he thought. He strode towards the central desk, followed by the children and Crane. His voice, when he spoke, was loud and clear. There would be no hissing with the mask.

"Good morning. I am Morgan Fletcher."

The woman at the desk looked startled, as the guard had done, then scared. Her eyes opened wide, as though stretched from within. "I'm sorry?" she said. She stared behind him towards the door, perhaps to make sure that he had been allowed in by someone and was not a mere intruder.

"I am Morgan Fletcher and I should like to see my sister," Morgan said.

"Your sister?" the woman said.

Morgan stepped back and glanced along the row of desks, behind each of which a woman gaped, appalled, in his direction. He felt the presence of the guards behind him, gathered by the glass doors at the entrance to the foyer. "Is anyone among you capable of announcing my arrival to my sister? Rebecca Fletcher?" he said in a voice that echoed in the empty space. He thrilled to the sound of it, the clear pure sibilance of *sister*. One of the women to his left gave a shrill, nervous laugh. He walked towards her and paused in front of her desk. She was young; her hair was pulled back from her face into a metal clasp, reflected in the mirror behind her head, as Morgan was, and the Doctor, and the heads of the children, with Mite still in Melissa's arms. Nothing will happen to you, he thought. I will make sure of that. The metal clasp was in the form of the letter *F*, Morgan noticed. He smiled at his face in the polished glass. I can frighten you, he thought, because I am powerful and a word from me could have you fired, and you know that. Just imagine if you saw my face. Then you would know what fear was and you would think it was pity.

"Perhaps you can help me?" he said. He heard himself speak, a model of courtesy. How proud his mother would have been of him. Or maybe not; courtesy wasn't her style. The blood drained from the woman's lips. She shook her head, then nodded. "Of course. I'll tell the director general you're here," she whispered, dry-mouthed with shock. She stood up and walked around her desk, before breaking into a knock-kneed run towards a broad flight of stairs to Morgan's left. He smiled and leant across the desk to pick up the receiver of a square black telephone with his good hand. "Wouldn't it be simpler to use this?" he said. "I imagine my sister also has a telephone." The woman halted and scuttled back. After a moment's hesitation, she took the receiver from him, pressing a number on the telephone, her knuckles white. But why this fear, wondered Morgan, because there was no sense to it that he could see. Yet he revelled in it too. He would have liked to whistle or make some low gruff animal noise or lash out like a cat with his wounded hand, simply to observe the effect. He was both ashamed of this desire and exhilarated. The woman had turned her back to them and was muttering into the receiver. Her conversation ended, she turned and said in a stronger voice that he should take the directors' lift, pointing towards a double door to their right, of burnished bronze framed in marble and gilt, flanked by pairs of smaller, more modest doors. Morgan looked around his group. The Doctor was leaning on his closed umbrella, which had made a pool on the marble floor. The children were staring around them, openmouthed.

"David," Morgan said. "Fetch Goddie from the car. He won't want to come, I know, but you will persuade him. I don't want anyone left behind. We have work to do and it's best if we do it together."

David nodded and ran across the foyer, his steps echoing. At the door, he paused. The armed men fell apart to let him through.

"The director general is waiting for you," the receptionist said in an unexpectedly loud voice, from which she appeared to take courage. "You really ought to go at once." Her tone was both anxious and officious. "She mustn't be kept waiting."

"She has been waiting for years," Morgan said. "A few more minutes won't hurt."

David came in with a trembling Goddie, who glanced around himself with awe, his hand in the older boy's. Together now, they walked towards the lift. Someone must have pressed a button somewhere, because the bronze doors opened and they stepped into a wood-lined box the size of a small room. There was choral music playing from some hidden source and the air was heavy with a scent that was flowers and not flowers, a stultifying chemical essence. The doors closed behind them soundlessly, the lift began to rise. After no more than five or six seconds, marked only by the stifled whimpering of Goddie, the lift eased to a halt and the doors slid back to reveal a corridor wider than most rooms, with honey-coloured light falling onto carpets that reminded Morgan of his home. Low tables along the walls bore intricate Oriental vases and porcelain animals: lions, dragons; objects his grandfather might have collected, although he had never seen them before. It was natural, he thought, that she should do this; deprived of her own home as a child, she would do whatever she could to repossess it. They walked down the corridor towards an open door at its far end. Daisy had her arm round Goddie's shoulders. Then David said, "They recognized you downstairs with the mask on and that was good. It helped us get in. But you don't need it here. Not with your sister. She knows who you are."

Morgan flinched. His hands rose slowly to his face.

"You want me to take it off?" Morgan's fingers felt for the edge of the mask but it seemed to have disappeared, the surface of skin and wax was unfractured by any seam. Why should he take it off? he thought. Why should he expose himself to his sister?

"It isn't what I want," said David. "It's what you have to do."

"You don't need it," Crane said, resting his hand on Morgan's shoulder, giving it a squeeze. He treats me like a brother, thought Morgan, and yet I resent him for that as well, as though they were all my enemies, not only my long-dead mother and Rebecca, not only the uniformed men and women that protect her from the world as much as I am protected from the world by the walls around the house. But also the children, Engel, Crane. They were right, he knew, but how much it hurt to feel for the seam and ease the face that Morgan had begun to think of as his, as his real face, away from the thing that lay below, which was foreign to him. It had always been foreign. You can't grow into a face that was never yours, he thought. He thought of his own face as the mask and the mask as the true face that lay beneath it. And then he remembered Goddie, who had never seen the face beneath the mask and would be scared. But David was whispering to the smaller boy. He nodded at Morgan. Now, his mouth said, and Morgan lost sight of them all as the wax passed over his eyes, then, when he was naked and flinching at the air on his own skin, he saw that Goddie was not scared after all, but pitying and sad, and awed. Tears pricked his eyes.

"She's waiting," David said. He looked and sounded like a man. He continued, in a softer voice, "Don't worry. All you have to do is ask for Moira back. Ask her to take us there, where Moira is. See what she says. If she takes us, well and good. If she doesn't, we'll wait and see what she does. It doesn't matter either way. We'll get Moira back in any case." He cocked his head. "I think I can hear her. Listen."

They stood there silent. Morgan heard nothing, but Goddie and the other children nodded. "She's a long way off," said Goddie.

Then they heard the voice of a woman from beyond the open door.

# CHAPTER TWENTY-FIVE

*in which Morgan and Rebecca talk about power*

"Morgan? Is that you?"

"Yes, my dear," he said. He walked along the final stretch of corridor and into a room that was bare except for a vast white table and, behind it, the seated figure of his sister. She was looking away from them, towards a window, so they saw her profile first. A long nose, high forehead, her chin a little sharper than it should be. She was dressed in black, her blond hair scraped back from her face and twisted into a chignon. Her face was very fine, she had always been beautiful, he thought, and apparently there were no signs of ageing, although it was hard to tell at this distance. He walked towards her and watched her, to see what she would do. He wanted to see if she recoiled. She hadn't seen him, after all, since the clinic. Her memory might have made him worse, there was always that possibility. But she didn't react at all. She turned her head from the window and looked at him in her level way, which she had learned from their mother, and then glanced at the others. He saw a flicker of distaste on her lips and thought at once that this would not be for his own children but for Goddie, still whimpering a little. She had never liked rough boys, or crybabies. Or perhaps it was Mite, because, so far as he knew, Rebecca had never had a baby, or even a pet. She had hated and feared their mother's dogs, he remembered that well enough. With a shiver, as though a blanket had been torn away from him, he felt that he and his sister were children again, in the rose garden or hiding among the yew bushes, with their mother bearing down on them, her dogs behind her, and Rebecca ready to cry and blame him for something, and his mother ready to spring to his defence. That was why his mother had tried to kill him, to take him with her. She hadn't loved Rebecca enough for that, they would know this always, both of them. They would always know, apart from everything else, her power, his pain, that his wounded face was a sign of their mother's special love.

"You've come all this way, Morgan," she said. "What on earth for?"

"You know why I've come," he said.

"Do I?" She looked behind him. "You aren't alone, I see."

"These are my friends."

"How wonderful to have friends," she said. "Friends are people who accept you for what you are, isn't that so? That's what I've been told. Who appreciate you." She smiled. "I see you surround yourself with children."

"Rebecca," Morgan said. This was a word he could say, he realized. How strange that, among the names he could still pronounce, there should be that of his sister. "Some people took a child of mine. A girl child called Moira."

"Yes?"

"We think she's here," he said. "We think you have her."

"You'd like her to be here, I know that. How simple everything would be if we could always have what we want. But then, that's what you've always had, isn't it? Everything you want."

"How can you say that?" Morgan gestured towards his face.

Rebecca laughed, scornful. "Oh, that," she said. "There are worse things that can happen in the world than that. You have no idea how wicked the world can be, Morgan."

Morgan remembered what David had written on the blackboard in the schoolroom, about the world's wickedness. Before he could speak, he felt David move beside him. The boy took his hand. He spoke in his high clear voice.

"You know she's here. This is where all the children end up when they're taken away from their homes and disappear. Where else would she be?"

Behind them, Goddie cried out, "I want to go."

"Take that brat out of here," Rebecca snapped.

Morgan walked towards her until his face was only feet from hers. He saw, with an unexpected thrill, his sister shrink back. He lifted a corner of his top lip, knowing full well the effect this had. For a moment, her hand rose, as though she wanted to cover her own mouth or reach out to caress what was left of his, her expression an unresolved conflict of pity and repulsion.

"What took you so long, Morgan?" she said. "I've waited for you to come. I've wanted to talk to you, often, to see how you were. I've driven to the gate, you know that? And looked into the garden and wondered. And driven away."

"I never drove you away."

"I sent that woman to you, the one who insisted so much."

"Engel?"

"Was that her name? She turned up in my office one day, God only knows how. She said you needed her. I thought you would see for yourself if that was true or not. She wouldn't take no for an answer, I remember that. I thought she might tell me herself what was happening in the house, become a sort of spy, I suppose, but that didn't happen. I never saw her again."

"She's still with me," Morgan said.

"I did the right thing then?"

"Yes."

"Why is that child whining?" she said. Morgan turned to see Goddie crouched on the floor, as if he'd been kicked. He said in a low voice to David, "Comfort him." David knelt beside him, to stroke his hair.

"What are you doing here?" Morgan asked, turning back to his sister.

She looked startled.

"Doing?"

"This place. This factory. What does it do?" He'd told David the factory made power, and David had nodded, but even now he knew nothing of the factory's purpose. He'd never wanted to know, which is also a sort of knowing.

Rebecca laughed. "What a fool you are, Morgan. You think because you've suffered you're exempt from responsibility, but you're wrong. What's made in this factory puts food in your mouth and clothes on your back as much as it does mine. You're as guilty as I am, if that's what you imagine me to be. You'd prefer me to be guilty for you perhaps?"

"Rebecca," Morgan said, "I want my child."

"Your child? They're all your children, I suppose, all the poor lost infants of the world. All struggling to find a place under your wing. Somewhere safe and warm and innocent." She sat up straight in her chair, which rose behind her head like a throne in a tale. "And what do you think we do with children here that's so awful? So unimaginable? Do you think we torture them, or eat them? The children are our raw material, Morgan. We make them work for their keep. The world is built on work, Morgan, didn't you know? What do you think the others do, your maids, your gardeners, that woman Engel, you think they work for the love of you, for the love of work? How stupid you are. Isolation has addled your brain."

She turned her head once again to the window. Morgan felt sick with humiliation as he stood there, because everything she had said was true. He waited for her to continue, as though his final purpose here were to be punished.

But David would have none of it.

"You don't work any more than he does," he said, with contempt. "Your strength comes from the strength of others. You sit up here and boss people round, you don't even see what they do. If you did, you'd be ashamed. You think you're safe but you aren't. No one is. Morgan's a good man, and that's *his* work, to be good. We'd all be dead without him. You aren't so special. You've no more right to live than anyone else."

"That's enough, David," said Morgan. "My sister knows what she is saying." He looked at her, the pale set face framed by the leather of the chair back, like the perfect head of a doll on a shelf. "We've neither of us had children," he said. "It isn't surprising, I know that. But we must still learn how to live."

She sprang up from the chair. She was as tall as he was, taller than David. She walked round to the front of the table and Morgan struggled not to fall back to avoid her. When she was close enough to touch him, her hand went up to his cheek, the wounded one. She stroked it once, he felt her fingernails against him, then turned towards the door.

"You can have your Moira, but you must leave me one to replace her. I have to balance my books." She pointed at Goddie. "That one will do."

Goddie moaned. A puddle of piss appeared between his feet.

"I'll stay," said David.

"Wait," said Crane. "This woman has no right to dictate conditions."

Rebecca laughed.

"I see your adult friend also has a voice," she said to Morgan. "Perhaps he is more than your friend. You have found your consolation there."

Morgan shook his head.

"Crane is right. This place belongs as much to me as it does to you."

Rebecca laughed. "Belongs to you? And what have you ever done for this?"

But David insisted. "Let me stay here." He stepped forward and bent his head before Rebecca. "You can have me. I'm stronger than a baby girl and I'll work harder. You won't regret it." He glanced across at Goddie, his lip curling. "He's no good, just look at him. He's weak and scared, he'll do nothing but cry and wet himself." He stared up into her eyes. "Take me."

She swivelled on her heels and walked to a door. It opened as she approached and a woman appeared, dressed as the women in the foyer had been dressed. This woman must have been listening and waiting. When she saw Morgan, she gasped and turned her face away.

"Bring me the child. You know the one they mean." She beckoned David towards her. He looked at Morgan, who tried to hold his arm, to protect him, and nodded, as if to say, Leave me alone, I know what I'm doing. Morgan stepped back. "And have this boy taken down to the reception area."

"No," said David. "I want to see where she's kept, where they're all kept. Otherwise I won't stay."

Rebecca looked impressed. "You're quite the little man, you know that, don't you?" She looked at Morgan, with feigned pity. "How can you bear to lose him?" Morgan paled. "How many have you got? Thirty? Forty. I heard you had forty-four. Surely that can't be true?"

"Take us to the children," he said. How did Rebecca know? Was Engel a spy, after all?

She nodded slowly, then waved a hand to dismiss the woman, who hurried from the room.

"Very well," she said. "If anyone has a right to see them, you do. We'll go together."

She led them out of the room and down a second, less opulent, corridor. Everywhere there was silence. It seemed that no one else was alive in the building, no one but this odd group, the striding woman and her disfigured brother in the lead, the children and the Doctor following. The only sound was the click and shuffle of their heels against the tiles and the constant snuffling of Goddie. All the light came from above, there were no windows, and Morgan wondered where they were in relation to the world outside. They must be walking along the spine of the factory, he thought, otherwise they would already have reached an external wall and been forced to turn. How long the building was he could only imagine. Driving alongside it they had passed a mile, perhaps more, of various structures but now, if he was not mistaken, they were pushing further on, into a part that he had not seen. They walked for long minutes, he couldn't tell how many, before they came to some glass doors, behind which was a flight of stairs. They followed Rebecca down the stairs. They glanced through further sets of doors and saw the life of the building framed beyond them, workers at machines, offices, a kind of showroom. Daisy was dragging her feet by now and began to say that she was tired and what was the point of all this, why couldn't David have gone by himself and where was Moira anyway? She handed Mite over to the Doctor, who took the baby with relief, as though the presence of that small sleeping body in his arms would reassure him. Morgan's fingers were fidgeting with the face in his pocket, he wanted to put it on before anyone else could see him as he was. He still felt shaken by the reaction of the woman in Rebecca's office. It had been so long since someone had gasped with horror at the sight of him; he had forgotten what it was like to be feared. He pulled the thing out and was about to lift it to his face when David saw him. "No, don't do it," he said urgently. "Not now. You'll need it later. You'll know when. Save it for when it counts." And Morgan, who had begun to understand the economy of the mask, slipped it back into his pocket.

At the bottom of the stairs were two steel doors. Rebecca touched a panel and they opened.

# CHAPTER TWENTY-SIX

*in which Morgan and the others reach the potting shed*

Outside the doors was a narrow garden, with coarse blue-green grass cut short like a lawn, and beyond that a vast windswept field. Slabs of concrete set into the grass led along this side of the garden to a low structure about a hundred yards away, not much taller than a grown man. At first glance, the walls of the structure seemed to be made of vegetation. But as they approached, they saw that netting had been suspended from a metal frame, and camouflaged. From above, the structure would have been invisible; from where they stood, it resembled a greenhouse of sorts, whose function was to protect what grew from the light, from the world outside. As they entered, passing beneath a lifted flap, the dim green light stretched out as far as the eye could see.

Morgan's sight was fading so what he saw at first looked like an endless field of turnips after the tractor had passed, turnip roots thrown over by the blade, dirt-brown, dirt-crimson, white where the steel had cut into them and split them open. But when he stooped to look more closely at the one nearest his feet, he saw that the white was the whimpering face of a child and the bare flayed stalks its arms and hands. "Oh, my poor dear," he said, his voice breaking with shock. He bent to take the child to him—boy or girl, he wasn't sure—and succour it in some way. But the earth resisted. He dug until the neck and the frail soft sweep of the shoulders were visible. The earth was poor, stony: he broke a nail and felt a stab of pain. Behind him he could hear the others, Crane, David, Rebecca, and other voices he didn't recognize, but he had no time to spare. Slowly he uncovered the tops of the arms. He wanted to slide his hands beneath the armpits and lift the child up, ease it away from soil to be held. But the child's face changed as Morgan worked. Anxiety swept across it. Morgan struggled to grasp the child—a girl, he was sure of it now—to hold and raise it, as if from the dead. The girl's head began to shake, her mouth opened as if to speak. "We're nearly there," soothed Morgan. "We're nearly there."

"No, wait," said David. "I think we might hurt them. They've been here too long. We have to find the others. There must be others somewhere."

"You can do nothing here, Morgan," said Rebecca, standing a short way away from him, her arms folded.

"What is this evil place?" he said, his voice trembling, the hissing of the sibilants terrible.

"We call it the potting shed," said Rebecca. "We had one at home, you must remember it."

"This can't be true," he said, shaking as he tore at the soil, at the white flesh of the girl.

"Of course it's true. It's what we are. Surely you know that, by now. Your little errand of mercy."

But Morgan was on his knees, his hands caked with dirt, his split nail bleeding; he had the girl within his grasp. Her head was pressed to his chest as he straightened up and felt her loosen, slowly at first and then, with a strange wet noise, in a rush. He fell back as the girl came free.

"I told you," said David. "I told you not to do it."

# CHAPTER TWENTY-SEVEN

in which David works a miracle

Morgan let himself be led out of the potting shed, away from the broken child. He was stumbling, shocked into silence by the horror of what he had done.

"You mustn't feel bad," said David, stroking his arm. "It wasn't your fault. Your sister knew what would happen if you kept pulling. She could have told you. She wanted you to learn the hard way."

"The hard way is the only way I have ever learned anything," said Morgan, as much to himself as to David.

"She thinks you'll change your mind once you see. It wouldn't have happened otherwise. She doesn't plan to give up that easily." He looked away. Morgan followed his eyes and saw Rebecca, standing at a distance, flanked by men in uniform, watching them both. She nodded slowly, as if she had heard David's words and concurred with them. Perhaps she had, and did. Of course she would want him to go back to the house and to his long, humiliating sleep. Maybe that was why Engel had been sent to him, it occurred to him. To keep him comfortable, and quiet. And there beside him was this field, this interminable field, the small heads breaking the surface of the soil and the noise they made, a pulsing intermittent moan, rising and falling as one, as though they had found this way of being together. Because the potting shed was only the start of it all. There was no end in sight.

"Give what up?" he said.

"Well, you'll have to give it up as well, of course," said David. "But you know that, don't you?"

Morgan nodded. "I want no part of this."

"But this is what you are," said David. "As much as she is. You can't pick and choose, you know."

"You're here to take this from me?"

"You aren't so important, Morgan," said David with an unexpected smile. "Neither am I. Now that you know. It's what we do now that matters, not what we are."

"How could I have saved the life of that poor child?"

"You can't save everyone, Morgan. Nobody can."

"I wasn't trying to save everyone," said Morgan. "Just her. Can't we do that too? I mean, save people one by one?" As Crane has saved me, he thought. Crane and Engel, and you, David, all of you. As all of you have saved me. One by one, my oneness saved, and for what? For what we do.

David took his hand, the hand with the broken fingernail. "Let me look at that," he said. He touched it, then wrapped his own hand round the nail and closed his eyes. A moment later the pain had gone.

"You work miracles," said Morgan. "I thought so."

"Well, some people call them that," said David.

"I have to get away from this," said Morgan. He began to cross the field, eyes focused on his feet as they picked their way along a path that led through the dreadful crop all round him, Melissa and the others a few steps behind.

# CHAPTER TWENTY-EIGHT

*in which the children are freed*

By the time they reached the far side of the field, Rebecca and her silent guards could hardly be seen through the misting fall of rain. Morgan was exhausted. He had almost ceased to notice the ground beneath his feet and what it held. So it came as a surprise to him when David touched his arm.

"Here," he said, pointing down to their left. "We can start here." He knelt beside a small blond head, its eyes closed, the face turned up to the light, and began to clear the soft damp earth away from the neck. "Come on," he said, with a child's impatience. "You start on that one." He nodded along the line. Morgan saw that Crane had also begun to scrape at the soil ten yards further down, Melissa beside him. Beyond them stood Goddie, with Mite in his arms. He dropped to his knees.

"We'll soon have you out of here," he said. The face beneath him was different from that of the first child. It seemed unformed, more like a bud than a face, the skin across the eyes translucent; Morgan imagined—or saw, he wasn't sure—the pupils beneath, like small bright beads of light. The lips too seemed sealed. It startled, and thrilled him when he noticed as he dug a tremor around the mouth and the hesitant blossoming of a smile. His hands worked harder, until the child was free of earth to the waist, and then, because he could not bear the memory of the other, to the knees. This child was a boy, his genitals cupped by his palms. "Nearly there," said Morgan. "Nearly there." Kneeling beside him, David had already cleared a space and eased a girl out of the soil. The roots and all, thought Morgan, the image of the first girl in his head. And then he recalled something he'd read in one of his grandfather's bound magazines, the words of an artist who had travelled the world. Where are your roots? the artist had been asked, and he had answered, I am not a plant, I am a human being. Is this what is wrong with us, Morgan wondered, that we think we have roots and are bound to where we are?

And then his child was free. Morgan lifted him out of the hole he had made. Before his eyes, the skin, which had been as pale and delicate as the brittle skin of an onion, took on colour and depth and softness, and became human skin. The eyes opened, and then the mouth, and the smile which had been no more than the shadow of a smile was all at once complete. It's like a birth, thought Morgan. A human birth. David was wrong, he said to himself. One by one is the only way.

The child he had freed lay by the hole for a moment, gathering his strength, the skin above his heart a sort of glimmering sheen, and then, as though held by invisible hands, he rose to his feet, shaking the loose earth from his skin. He kissed Morgan's cheek before walking along the row and sinking to his knees to dig out a second child. Morgan looked round. The part of the field they had reached was alive with children, David and the girl he had freed, Melissa and Crane helping others to rise from the soil and fall to the work themselves. It's exponential, thought Morgan, one by one becoming two by four. One by two by four by eight is the only way, he said to himself. So David was right after all. And then into his head came another story from his childhood, about dragon's teeth that had been sown and an army that had risen from the ground, fully armed.

In the distance, where Rebecca had stood with her guards, was a line of uniformed men. "We need to hurry," he said.

# CHAPTER TWENTY-NINE

*in which Goddie finds himself*

By the time Rebecca and her men arrived, the children had been freed in the hundreds, naked as the day they were born, that other day before this day, that other birth before this second birth. It was hard to judge their age— some seemed infants, others almost adult—and Morgan wondered how much this mattered. They were alive, after all. He felt an exhilaration in his blood as he watched them moving around the field, their first few steps uncertain, like newborn deer, sizing one another up, as dogs would almost, a recognition that had to do with scent and feel, it seemed, that lay beyond words. Still, there were greetings too, and embraces, reunions, sometimes of siblings, at times of friends. The past was flowing back, to fill them up. All of this power, Morgan thought, returned to its rightful owners. Not everyone spoke the same language, he noticed. Standing beside him, Crane said, "Listen to them, chirruping like birds," and began to laugh, and Morgan laughed with him.

David was walking among them and it soon became clear that lines were being formed as he passed, lines of defence. The taller ones moved to the front, boys and girls alike, while the smaller ones fell back. Melissa had taken her place at the centre, with Mite, and with those too young to walk, who had found their home in some older child's arms. The uniformed men were closer now, thirty or forty of them, no more than that, Rebecca no longer with them. There was a ribbon, broad as a road, of upturned earth between the men and the children. David stood at the front, with Goddie by his side, both clothed, surrounded by the almost blinding whiteness of rain-damp skin. Morgan and Crane walked forward, to where they could watch both forces face off. Goddie was trembling, but fierce. David stared ahead. Morgan saw him as if for the first time, a man now, and was thrilled. He reached in his pocket for his face and pulled it out. It hung from his hand like a limp rag, formless. It had nothing to do with him, he thought; it belonged to the head in the house. He stroked it with his free hand before putting it away again.

"You don't need it," said Crane, who had been watching him.

"I realize that now," said Morgan.

That was when they heard the noise of the bullhorn. It came from the factory. As one, the men turned and walked away, towards the noise. The children began to murmur among themselves, until a cheer broke out from somewhere behind them, and spread through the crowd. Crane raised his arms in the air. It had stopped raining, and Morgan, looking up, saw the sun still high in the sky. It can't be much past noon, he thought. How quickly all this has happened. And then he remembered the child he had torn in half, and the potting shed, and felt sick with shame and disgust. This was no time to celebrate. He reached up and grabbed Crane's arm. "We must leave this place," he said.

David stepped forward, then turned to face his army. There were hundreds, tens of hundreds. Morgan saw that a dozen or more had slipped away to enter the potting shed, and wondered what they might be doing. But he was distracted by a whistle, and the clear high voice of David. He had started to sing, a wordless song, and everyone's eyes were on him as the two boys at his side moved closer and lifted him onto their shoulders. He sat between them, enthroned, his song an anthem, an incantation, the two boys rotating slowly with their charge until they faced the factory once more. They started to walk, with measured strides, and the nature of David's song was instantly transformed into a march. Slowly at first, and then in a rush, the other children joined in, their voices harmonious and tuneful, pitched with confidence as though the song were known to them already, and Morgan found himself also singing, words that were not words but that nonetheless had meaning to him, although what that meaning was he couldn't say, and would never know, however hard he tried. The song, its melody, would always elude him. There, in the upturned field, with the loose clods shifting beneath his feet, his chest filled with the roundness of it, his mouth seemed healed as he sang, the sibilance of certain consonants no obstacle to him. Crane too had begun to sing. He glanced across at Morgan as they moved to follow the children, to follow David, and raised an eyebrow, startled by what he saw.

Ahead of them, the orderly flock of children had reached the low sweep of the factory and were pouring through the doors, which had been opened wide to admit them, by whom Morgan didn't know. Rebecca was nowhere to be seen. The uniformed men had disappeared, as Mill had when they came for Moira, thought Morgan, dissolved into thin air. And there was Mite now, held up in the air like a banner, only yards away from him. And all the babies were hoisted up with him, unfurled and chuckling, their small hands opening and closing, clutching at the ebb and flow of the song as it streamed around them. Moira was there as well, he saw, Moira without whom they might never have risked this journey. Moira, first born, first found, whose name means Fate. So everything has served its purpose. But surely it can't be this easy, he asked himself. Shall we simply walk away, this power unleashed and free to roam, the walls of the factory, like those of some ancient and now forgotten city, left to crumble around their own irrelevance? He was about to say this to Crane when a low roar came from the front of the group, already inside the factory, a roar that grew louder and deeper as it flowed back through the clamorous crowd of children, and seemed to flex itself, a roar as dense and blood-saturated as a muscle.

Long before he reached the factory doors, with the newly broken clods of damp earth shifting and rocking beneath his feet, Morgan had recognized the smell: the cloying sweetness of it, the underlying pungency. He had tasted it before, once in his life, in the back of his throat, but had never imagined he would be forced to taste it again. Instinctively, both hands rose to his face, to cover it, but also to protect his good eye from what it would see. Crane stood beside him, their shoulders just touching; he could feel the man's presence as a source of warmth, and comfort. But the comfort Crane could provide would not save him from the scene that met his eye. He paused at the doors, aghast. They were back in the atrium of the factory, but it was barely recognizable. The row of desks had been displaced, as had their occupants. The vast room was stained and tainted by blood, blood glistening on the infinite expanse of floor, blood splashed in great bright swathes across the walls. The windows above the open doors were washed in it, so that all the light was livid pink. The children, in their nakedness, were bathed and clothed in blood. They were standing still, or turning slowly on their heels, now cleansed of earth, their good work done.

And there, at the heart of the atrium, on one of the low sleek desks that had once lined the wall, was Goddie, naked like the others now, his oversize suit cast off, stark ribs sticking out beneath the skin as he raised one fist above his head and hollered in crazy glee. When he saw Morgan, the holler died away. Slowly, with a triumphant smile, he lowered his fist and furled the fingers back to reveal the metal clasp he'd been grasping, the pin sunk deep in his flesh, unbleeding, the letter *F* like a glittering worm in the middle of his palm.

# CHAPTER THIRTY

in which the road home is taken by some but not by all

The car followed the army back along the road it had taken that morning. But *army* no longer described what was now a straggling flock of children, in holiday mood, anarchic, darting to pick bramble fruit from the hedges, jumping over ditches to drink their fill of new-fallen rainwater from troughs and streams. There was a festive mood, an air of picnic, with David darting among them like a thoughtful sprite, applying his healing touch wherever it might be needed. One boy had found a bicycle and was giving the smaller children rides on the handlebars. Some children had wandered away, like homing birds, while others joined the group, running from houses and barns as if they had been hiding, or held against their will, and were finally released. Exposure to the sun had begun to colour the pasty white skin of those who had been lifted from the field. The country at each side of the road seemed greener than it had that morning, only hours before, although it didn't feel like that to Morgan. It felt as though the world he had known had been transformed as it had the day his mother had chosen to die, taking with her his own, unspoiled face just as surely as Goddie had ripped the clasp from the woman's head. Everything was fresh and new, it seemed to Morgan, and he wondered how this could be so, how this bloom of freshness was possible, with the image of the atrium still before his eyes.

At the control post they had passed through on their way to the factory, the barrier had been lifted before their arrival. News travels fast, thought Morgan. The soldier on guard was squatting on a stool with his shirt open, smoking a cigarette, watching the children go by. When he saw the Doctor, he smiled and waved a hand. The Doctor, unsmiling, nodded back. He hadn't spoken since they drove away from what remained of the factory. Before they began their journey he had walked across the fractured earth to the potting shed, or what was left of it, but when Morgan asked him what he had found there, he shook his head. He sat with his hands in his lap, staring ahead as the car made its way towards the house. The children continued before them, untiring, occasionally stopping in their onward movement to play some complex game, a weaving in and out, arms raised and lowered, without any visible leader, like bees, thought Morgan. The car had almost come to a halt behind one of these games, when the Doctor spoke.

"They dug them in," he said. "They dug them back into the earth."

"Who did?"

"Your sister's men."

"How do you know that?" Morgan remembered what he had seen: a dozen children leaving the group to enter the potting shed.

"I knew one of them. He was a patient of mine some years ago, he'd broken his arm in a brawl. He pretended not to know me. He was hiding behind the shed, from me

I thought at first, but he must have been hiding from the children, surely. After what he'd seen them do. He must have been hiding from the children. He might have thought I meant him harm as well, of course. For a moment, with what I'd seen still in my head, I did. The earth was moving beneath my feet, Morgan, there were fingers pushing through," he said, his voice breaking. He hid his face in his hands.

Morgan waited for him to continue. One of the girls nearest the car had gathered poppies from a field and was plaiting them into another girl's hair. The girl whose hair was adorned bent down her head and stared into the car. She saw Morgan, Morgan's face as it was, and Morgan expected her to recoil, flinched with anticipation, but her face was alive with welcoming laughter and a craving to be admired. Morgan stared back, but couldn't smile.

"I asked him what he thought they had done," the Doctor said in the end. "He didn't answer me. He didn't seem to see the point of my question. Can you understand that, Morgan? He didn't see the point. I lost my temper with him then, I shook him and he let me do it, he was limp in my hands. I had no choice, he said. It's what we were told to do." Crane turned to face Morgan, urgent now. "Is that all we are, Morgan? Tools at the service of power? Unquestioning tools? I *trod* on them, Morgan, they were struggling, stifled with earth, beneath my feet, I couldn't help it. I tried to pull one out and the same thing happened to me as had happened to you. He broke in my hands like a stalk. What dreadful power did they produce that this should have been done to them?" He grasped Morgan's shoulder until

Morgan winced. "You knew nothing of this? Tell me you knew nothing of this, Morgan. I need to be told you had no hand in this."

"I think I've been chosen," said Morgan after a moment. "And I don't know why. At first, I thought it was because I'd suffered and that would help me understand the suffering of others, of the children, certainly, but of more than that, I don't know how to say it. Some larger suffering. But now I begin to think I was chosen because I am guilty. And then I thought, perhaps to be made whole, you must first be broken. I said something to Melissa once, long ago now, after they'd found the woman. You know they call her their mother? I heard them once. All of them together, like worshippers. But why are you here? I asked her. Are you here to help me or am I here to help you?" The children themselves went into the potting shed, thought Morgan, what Crane has seen is the work of the children. No one is innocent.

"And what did she say?"

Morgan shrugged. "She told me I'd missed the point. David had said something similar to me already, before that day." He shook his head, then sighed. "It seems I'm doomed always to miss the point. Today I feel that I have seen what I am capable of doing, perhaps of what I have done, or allowed to be done in my name, and I don't know how I would go on if I didn't have this girl looking in at the window, her hair filled with poppies." He turned to face the Doctor, raising a hand to stroke his cheek. "Do you feel this touch, Crane? Do you feel what it has done?"

Morgan was interrupted by a gentle tapping at the window. He wound it down. Goddie stood there, a chain of daisies around his neck, dressed in nothing but a soldier's jacket and grinning from ear to ear.

"I wanted to say goodbye to you before I went," he said. "My home is over there." He pointed towards a cottage in a field.

"But we found you in the city," said Morgan.

Goddie looked stubborn for a moment, his small face set, then grinned again, as though what Morgan had said was, after all, immaterial. "Thank you," he said, "for what you did." On an impulse, he reached into the car and touched Morgan's twisted mouth with his hand, the lightest touch and yet Morgan felt it, as warmth on his deadened skin. How strange, he thought, first one touch and then another, as though we could all be warmed back by the passing heat of others into some sort of decent life. When Goddie stepped back from the car, Morgan saw that the soldier's jacket was held closed across the boy's thin chest by the woman's metal clasp, in the form of the family's initial. So everything will find its purpose in the end, he thought. He wondered what his grandfather would have said.

As the road wound its way through open countryside, other children fell away from the procession, in groups or couples, sometimes with a smaller child between them as though they had already formed a family, less often singly, heading off towards houses and barns or any place that offered them shelter. Most of them had found clothes of some sort by now. Among those who were left, the babies were passed from arm to arm, from shoulder to shoulder, piggyback riding as the ever-diminishing raggle-taggle army moved east and the sun sank lower in the sky to guide and greet them. By the time the wall, and then the gate, still open from that morning, came into sight no more than two score—thirty at the most—were left, a little weary and dragging their feet, and it was twilight.

# CHAPTER THIRTY-ONE

*in which Engel tells Morgan about the elements*

Engel was standing at the front door to the house, under the porch, her apron on, surrounded by the children who had remained at the house. When the first group arrived, she threw open her arms. "You must be starving," she cried, then turned to her own children. "Don't just stand there," she said. "Welcome them to your home." Shyly at first, they obeyed her, the two groups mingling together in the shade of the porch. After a few moments, she ushered them into the house, shaking her head at the state of the new arrivals. The minute David reached her, she hugged him close and whispered some words in his ear. He pulled away with a laugh. "It won't be long now," he said, and Engel nodded. "Everything in its own good time," she said. Morgan, who had left the car and was walking up the steps, heard this and wondered what it might mean. Crane took his arm; he had barely spoken again after Goddie had left them. Morgan sensed an absence in him, as though some secret vessel within him had been opened and its contents emptied out. Together, they stood beneath the porch until the drive was empty, then followed the children into the hall. Engel was leading them all through the green drawing room into one of the rooms that overlooked the garden. She opened the French windows with a flourish, then stood back. On the lawn beyond, long trestle tables had been set up and laid with food. From where he stood, Morgan could see boiled eggs arranged in glistening pyramids, sandwiches the size and shape of dominoes, deep bowls of fruit, pies and sausages small enough to be eaten in one go, carafes of juices, coloured jellies. The children surged through the French windows into the garden. He turned to Engel, now standing beside him, arms crossed on her bosom.

"You were expecting us," said Morgan. Together, with Crane behind them, they left the house and stood at the edge of the lawn.

She sighed with satisfaction as the children began to eat. Some stayed at the tables, reaching for whatever took their fancy. Others carried food off, held to their chests, as though afraid they might be deprived of it. Some helped each other, others turned their shoulders to their neighbour like a shield to ward off threat. One boy picked up a jug and tipped the juice into his mouth as if he had never drunk before, rivulets of orange liquid staining his chin and neck. "I've been expecting this for an age," she said. "A long age, longer even than mine."

He was used to not quite understanding Engel.

"We've been to the factory," he said.

"I know where you've been," she said, "and what you've done."

"David told you, I suppose," he said.

She must have heard the trace of irony in his voice. "And if he did?" she said. "What of it?"

"And so we have Moira back."

She nodded. "Yes, what counts is that we're all together

now. Even the ones that were missing are finally here with us. We can do what we have to do at last."

Crane had been listening to this. "Dear God. What more must be done?" he said. It was clear from the weariness of his tone that what he expected was for more horror to be committed.

"Air and fire and earth," she said. She seemed to be reading the words from some card, suspended before her, that only she could see. "Those trials are over now, thank the Lord. What's left is water, and water is the sweetest one of them all."

"I don't understand," said Crane. He sounded annoyed now, as if Engel were toying with him.

"Air?" said Morgan, throwing a warning glance at Crane.

She stared at Morgan for a moment, her eyes vacant. Had she forgotten who he was? he wondered. Then she shook herself.

"Some air is very bad, unbreathable. It stays in the lungs forever, even when nothing more can be done. When the throat is closed and the nails are broken and the lungs are dead. When everything is dead, there is still the air. It settles. You don't know what it's like. I pray you'll never know." She touched the unfeeling part of his face, for the first time, he realized later, when it would never be possible again. Her hand was cool, and hard. "You've known the presence of fire, of a sort, Morgan. You've known what the burning can do. And so have I."

"And then there is earth," said Crane. He turned away from them both and walked back into the house.

❀    ❀    ❀

Later that evening, when the new children had been shown around the house, David came into Morgan's study. He and Crane had been playing backgammon in a rackety, distracted fashion, to take their minds off the day behind them. Such a day, thought Morgan. Crane might have helped him understand the sense of it all, but he sensed that Crane was as lost as he was, perhaps even more so. It would take time, he decided, before the two of them could talk about the day's events. But the need to examine them in some way was impellent in Morgan, before whose eyes floated brutal images of his sister, of broken earth, of death, of a metal clasp that stood for him, that represented him, and of sights he had seen with his mind's eye only, too terrible to be described. So the arrival of David came as a release. Even more so when David took Morgan's arm and lifted him bodily from where he was sitting, his strength surprising, knocking the game table so that the board flipped over, the pieces sliding into Crane's lap. Morgan found himself standing beside the boy, as tall as he was now. How long has this been true, he wondered. How quickly this has happened. David took his hand, the wounded hand, and led him from the room. Morgan turned to look at Crane, who was gathering the pieces and stacking them in a pile, not looking at either of them.

"He must come too," said David, tilting his head towards the other man. "He's part of this." Morgan didn't expect Crane to obey the boy, but Crane stood up and followed them both, the boy leading Morgan, along the corridor to the Doctor's room. "Do you remember?" David said when the three of them were standing together at the centre of the room. "We were looking for something in here and we couldn't find it? And I was angry?" He looked at Morgan, who hadn't understood. "You weren't here, Morgan. It was the day we showed the Doctor the woman, do you remember, Doctor Crane?"

"Yes, I remember."

"Well, we were looking in the wrong place. We all thought it was something medical we needed, something we could see and touch, but we were wrong. We needed to know where we came from, you see. When we found the woman, and found out how to open her, we thought she might have been our mother, but we were wrong about that too. Our mothers are dead, all of them. We found out the truth in a story."

David crossed the room and knelt down to take something from the bottom shelf. It was a bound volume of magazines Morgan's grandfather had collected. Morgan remembered it from his childhood. They were stories of other worlds, of other planets, of visitors from other places, illustrated sometimes, but the illustrations were nothing compared to the pictures in Morgan's head. He had scared himself out of sleep with some of the tales the volume contained. David was crouched on the floor with the book in front of him, flicking through the pages in search of something. Finally, with a sigh, he stopped. "Here it is," he said. He picked the volume up and laid it on the Doctor's table. The two men stepped forward and began to read where his finger rested.

❀   ❀   ❀

For the first two years of the war, the Children's Home was a place of safety. Protected by a fortuitous combination of slipshod administration, good fortune and remoteness from the theatre of battle, the children led a peaceful, even idyllic life until the morning of March 6.

As the children settled down to drink hot chocolate around the long wooden tables of the refectory, three vehicles, two of them lorries, the other one an army jeep, pulled up in front of the home. Soldiers leapt from the jeep, entered the building and forcibly removed all forty-four children, hurling them onto the lorries like sacks of corn. When the housekeeper tried to protect the smallest child, little more than a baby, she was marched behind the Home and shot.

Following the raid, the shivering, frightened children were taken to a nearby town and held in the collection centre—a requisitioned factory—for almost two months, waiting for the first available train to leave for the camps in the East. The journey was long and bitter, but, when the train stopped to be refuelled or was shunted into a siding, singing could sometimes be heard from the freight car in which the children were held. Miraculously, deprived of food and with no more water than they had managed to carry with them concealed in their clothes, they all survived the week-long journey. On arrival in the East, forty-two of the children, some of them still too young to do more than toddle, were immediately gassed. The two oldest were put to death by firing squad within days of their arrival.

Soon after the morning raid, a telegram was sent to headquarters declaring that the Children's Home had been fumigated and that all trace of its residents had been removed.

# CHAPTER THIRTY-TWO

in which the boathouse reveals its purpose

David gathered the children together. It was night by now, the garden was pitch dark apart from the overlapping arcs of light from the windows of the house. Morgan, watching the scene from the porch, began to count them, but before he had finished they were crossing the lawn in a loose pack, talking and laughing among themselves, the youngest ones, as usual, in the arms or on the shoulders of the older children. They had eaten and bathed and found fresh clothes. There was an air about them of purity; that was the word that first came to Morgan, and that stayed with him. They had been washed clean. He wished Crane were with him, but the Doctor was still in his room, with the bound magazines open in front of him. All he would say was that this was nonsense, that it made no sense at all. He had refused to eat. Morgan had seen Crane's ashen face and the tremor of his hands. He is a doctor, and imagines he can heal the sick, but there are sicknesses no doctor can heal, Morgan told himself. He had seen Crane's power, which was the power to forgive as well as to heal. Let him be, said Engel, he'll be all right in the end. Morgan remained unconvinced of this, as perhaps did Engel. She has stayed in the house, thought Morgan, but a moment later he realized that he was wrong. He saw her scurrying across the lawn, the light from the windows reflecting on her white apron, like the tail of a rabbit in a torch beam.

It took Morgan some minutes to understand that David was leading the children towards the boathouse. Filled all at once with an anxiety he couldn't account for, he hurried after them. By the time he had caught up with the group, David had disappeared inside the building and turned on a light, which flooded out of the door and the side window onto the eager, smiling faces of the children. They were standing in a semicircle around the door, with Morgan and Engel behind them and to one side. David came out and beckoned Morgan. The children parted to let him through, until, once again, the two of them, Morgan and David, were alone inside the boathouse. The single light hung from the ceiling shone harshly into Morgan's good eye; for a moment he was blinded, and only the guiding hand of David prevented his falling into the lake as the water lapped by his feet.

"I want to thank you," said David.

"You have no need to thank me."

David shook his head, as if to dismiss this.

"Things will change now, because of what we did today. You know that, don't you?"

"I hoped that would be the case," said Morgan.

"No, not just at the factory," said David. "Here, too. Your life, this house. Nothing can stay the same any longer. I didn't expect this, none of us did. We didn't ask ourselves about what might happen here, I suppose. Perhaps we should have done." He paused, then shook his head. "It will be hard for you, I think."

"My sister is dead," said Morgan.

"There are other people," said David. "But yes, your sister is dead, and it will take a little time before the others pick up where she left off. I thought it might be different here, but all your books tell me something else, that nowhere is different, in the end." He smiled suddenly. "But we have made a difference, haven't we, Morgan? Today? Did you see their faces? When we took the factory from them? Did you see what they understood in the end? That it was over? For a while at least."

"Doctor Crane is too shocked to speak."

David shrugged. "He's a doctor, isn't he? Doctors ought to be at home with blood. Where we come from, doctors used us for worse than that. It's all in your books, even when they pretend it isn't true and call it stories. You saw that. Sometimes that's all you can do with the truth. You should go and look."

"You're more of a man than Crane is," said Morgan. "Sometimes, I've seen it in his face, the way he flinches. He's no better than a boy. It isn't his fault." He stared down into the water. "You've noticed that too, David, I know you have. I've seen you lose your patience with him."

David nodded. "Death shocks him still. He thinks it doesn't, but it does. He has to get used to it. You should help him. You will know what to do. He thinks he's seen everything, but you know more than he does."

Morgan looked around him. "My mother died here. An awful death."

"It's not such a bad place to die," said David. "I mean, there are worse places than this." He took Morgan's hand, the damaged one. "Before I go," he said, "I want to fix this." He started to move the fingers, one by one, bending them forwards and backwards as far as they would go. Morgan watched, feeling nothing at first, half fascinated, half afraid, as though the hand belonged to someone else. Then, as

David worked, a sort of tingling filled the hand, like heat beneath the skin. It took all of Morgan's strength not to pull the hand away. He was thinking, What do you mean, before you go? How can you go? But before he could speak, David had freed his hand and was resting a palm on Morgan's sightless, always-open eye.

"Just be still," the boy said in a soothing voice. And Morgan was still. "I'm not putting everything right," David said. "I just want to make it easier for you to live. What's happened to you is you, you can't change that. You found that out yourself, with the wax face, didn't you? You thought you could keep it on forever and then you didn't want to. I'm right, aren't I? It was like how we were with the woman. We thought she might matter to us, love us, I suppose."

Morgan nodded, too awed to speak as his eye took in light and the boy's touch moved down to his mouth.

"Sometimes you have to give up the easy thing and do the right one," said David finally, stepping back as if to examine his work. A moment later, he turned and walked away. He paused in the boathouse doorway, a silhouette, and spoke to the ring of illuminated faces outside. He saw them all, Moira and Melissa, Georgina and Georgie, Daisy and Christopher and Ruth, and Mite, children he had fed and nursed, whose tears and blood and snot he had wiped away. Behind them, at some distance, stood Crane, staring out across the lawn like someone who had seen his own death. His eyes caught Morgan's. He shook his head. Morgan was about to go to him, to hold him, but David caught his hand. "Not yet," he said. Morgan nodded, but pain snagged his heart when Crane raised his shoulders in a gesture of despair and walked away, skirting the dark walls of the house, moving in and out of the arcs of light from the windows, until he could no longer be seen.

"It's time we went back home," David said. Morgan saw Engel cover her face with both hands as the children glanced at one another. Mite started to laugh, the gurgling laugh of a baby filled with the joy of its own vast life ahead of it. David had released Morgan and moved away. But then, as if caught by an unexpected memory, he paused, and Morgan saw him smile. "We have to go now," he said to Morgan. "But Engel will stay with you. You'll be all right. She'll make sure of that. And you must think of the Doctor. The Doctor is your responsibility now." He hesitated for a moment. "We'll miss you," he said, in a voice so quiet he could hardly be heard.

Morgan watched them walk past him, one by one, into the water.

# CHAPTER THIRTY-THREE

*in which Crane and Morgan talk about travel and the sense of it*

The following day Morgan rose early, unrested, and wandered the house, shocked by the silence that greeted him, a silence that seemed to fill his ears. How pervasive the noise of the children must have been, he thought, for its absence to feel so deafening. Everywhere there were signs of them, doors open onto unmade beds, a doll that had once belonged to Melissa, a pair of cotton socks rolled into a ball and thrown into a corner. He walked around the rooms they had slept in, eaten in, studied in; rooms in which he had watched them and offered them comfort, or received it. He touched their chairs and tables and beds, imagining warmth. Everywhere, he found the weight of the emptiness unbearable, stifling, as though their departure had deprived the house of air as well as noise. The kitchen was bare and cold, Engel's bed unslept in, the curtains drawn. She must be somewhere, he thought; he couldn't bear her not to be there. Closing the door to her room, a room he had never before entered without her consent, he reassured himself. David had promised him she would stay.

Morgan's hand was healed; he moved his fingers, tremulous, against his cheek. David had left him that, and he was glad, and not only because he had a hand that worked; without that, he might have believed, in the barren hush of the house, that no one had ever lived there but him. That he had always been alone.

That was when he heard the noise. It came from a room he rarely used, the largest of the several sitting rooms on the ground floor. He was walking past, his heels loudly echoing on the marble floor, when he heard what sounded like a sniffle. His heart leapt in his chest. They've come back, he thought. They've come back to me. He stepped into the room, ears cocked. The sniffle was repeated, once, twice, a third time. It came from behind the Chinese screen standing to the left of the fireplace. He walked towards it as quietly as he could, grateful for the deep pile of the Persian carpet beneath his feet, until he was close enough to take one edge of the painted screen in his hand. Now, he said to himself, and moved the screen to one side.

Crane was seated, cross-legged, on the floor, in the clothes he had been wearing the previous day. He looked up. He didn't seem surprised. "Hello," he said, his voice thick. "I wondered when you'd find me."

"Get up from there, Crane," said Morgan, more brusquely than he had intended. Resisting the urge to help his friend, he stood back to watch while Crane struggled to his feet. He felt an anger he did not understand.

"This is where you hid from me, isn't it?" said Crane, wincing a little as he shook the cramp from his leg. "The first time I came, for Daisy."

"How do you know that?" said Morgan.

Crane shrugged. "I don't remember. I expect Engel told me. Perhaps you gave yourself away." Both hands on his hips, he arched his back, twisted twice at the waist. "I must have been sitting down there too long," he said. He'd stopped sniffling, but his cheeks were still shiny with tears.

"I've been looking for you," said Morgan, although he wasn't sure how true this was.

"Well, now you've found me," said Crane. "Perhaps it isn't such a good place to hide after all." He paused. "Although it served its purpose for you, I suppose. When you thought you had to hide from me."

Morgan turned away, unsettled. Had he needed to have the children back so deeply that no other presence would do? Without them there would have been no Crane at all. He would be grateful, he decided; he would learn to be grateful. "You must be hungry," he said, his tone more generous. "We both need to eat. I imagine there will be something left from last night."

"Last night," echoed Crane, taking Morgan's arm in his as they walked across the sitting room. Nothing more was said until they were halfway down the stairs towards the kitchen, when Crane pulled him to a halt. "We can't just go on," he said, "as if nothing has happened."

"I don't intend to," said Morgan.

Engel was in the kitchen, her baking apron on, her hair pinned up inside her cap, kneading a ball of dough. She showed no surprise; she seemed to have been waiting for them to arrive. She nodded a welcome, then wiped her hands to pour out coffee from the jug into two cups, which she placed on the table. Morgan picked his up, more grateful than he could say. We are all still here, he thought. David was right. He didn't ask Engel where she had been.

"Excellent coffee," said Crane. He sat down. "As always, Engel."

"And why shouldn't it be?" said Engel, but her smile

belied the irritation of her words. She began to work the dough once more, tipping a cloud of flour from a small jute sack.

So already Crane was wrong, thought Morgan, cradling his coffee in his hands. We are, after all that has happened, to pretend that nothing has happened. Despite ourselves and what we know, this is what we shall do in order to be safe, to move on. We shall wipe out the last few days, the last few months, from our minds, our lives, as though we were blackboards and the children chalk. He put down his cup and traced a line in the film of flour on the table. A line, and then a letter. *M*.

That was when Crane noticed his hand. He put his own coffee down beside Morgan's and reached across to touch it as it wrote. Morgan flinched involuntarily, then let himself be held. He felt the slow heat of the other man on the new skin.

"How did this happen?" said Crane.

"David," said Morgan.

"David the healer," said Crane.

"He cured my eye as well," said Morgan, blinking. "You see? And listen, you hear my speech? I no longer lisp."

"David. The worker of wonders."

"Yes."

Crane shook his head, exasperated. "So why not work wonders all the time? Why not simply wave his magic wand and fix the world? He could have done so much."

"Perhaps it had to be done the hard way," said Morgan.

"Well, he put us through it," said Crane. "He certainly did

that." He continued to stroke the back of Morgan's restored hand, in a slow, distracted way, and Morgan allowed himself to relax into the pleasure of it.

Covering the ball of dough with a tea towel, Engel put a plate of shelled hard-boiled eggs on the table, a bowl of salt, a basket of bread. With his free hand, Crane dipped an egg into the salt and bit off the top half. He chewed for a moment. "I've been thinking all night and all I can do is come back to the same thought." He dipped the remaining half of the egg into the salt and ate it slowly; when he'd finished, a flake of yolk was left at the edge of his lower lip. "It's a scene, I suppose, and a feeling I can't quite fathom." He started to shake. At first Morgan thought he was laughing. He wanted to flick the yolk away, but the hand he needed was in Crane's hand. Then he saw that Crane had begun, once again, to cry. "He came away in my grasp," he stuttered through his tears. "That child. I killed him. If he was alive, and I don't even know that he was, I can't be sure of that, I killed him." He sucked back tears into his throat. "And so did you. You did it too." Pushing Morgan's hand to one side with a gesture of impatience, he twisted in his chair until he could take his friend by his shoulders and hold him close, so close Morgan felt the heat of Crane's breath on his face. "And I felt such disgust. Such disgust and horror, and sickness with myself. But I also felt a sort of freedom, do you understand that? As though I'd torn *myself* into two. Not the child, do you see? Myself." Crane wanted an answer, but all Morgan could do was stare into his eyes until he had finished with weeping and was still. And then, with a smile that Crane, he knew, would recognize as a smile, he said, "You have egg yolk on your lip," and he brushed it off.

"I can't go back to where I was," said Crane.

"You can stay here, in that case," said Morgan, his voice low, wilfully misunderstanding. He turned to Engel. "He can stay here with us, Engel, can't he? There's more than room enough."

Some hours later, during which they had wandered around the house and garden, arm in arm, in silence, the two men came to the main library. Crane said that he wanted to show Morgan something, and pulled open a shallow drawer, filled with hand-drawn and coloured maps. "Look," he said, lifting the first one out and carrying it across to the table at the centre of the room. "These must have been made by your grandfather."

"Or by someone for him," said Morgan, perversely.

"Well, that doesn't matter," said Crane. He was more himself now, as though not just the walking together but the crying fit of the morning had washed something loose in him and rinsed it out. "I was looking at them a few days ago, before we went out in the car, and it set me thinking about those books we were given to read as children, about travellers and shipwrecked sailors. How they found themselves in strange lands. Magical lands where time went backwards or animals spoke their language. But they weren't strange or magical to the people who lived there, were they? The people who lived there were normal. How formless it all is until an outsider gives it sense."

"I don't know what you mean."

"The children. They came out of thin air, that's what you said, isn't it? They came to do something we weren't expected, or entitled, to understand. I don't think they understood what they had to do themselves. And then David grew up somehow, so quickly, and it all fell into place. And now, here *we* are. We are what's left."

The longer he talked, the more animated he became. For the first time that day, he seemed happy, elated even. He lifted the map up from the table and replaced it in the drawer, eased out the one from beneath it and placed that where the first map had been. His finger traced a coastline, a bay, an inlet. He turned the map over so that nothing but the paper itself could be seen, with the faintest tracing where a nib had dug more deeply into the skin of it. "All these worlds we know nothing of," he continued. "They're all connected under the surface, I'm convinced of it. What doesn't happen in one place happens somewhere else. And at times the strangest things slip through."

"So somewhere the woman in the chest upstairs is giving birth to an actual child?" Morgan's tone was gently mocking.

"Exactly!" Crane clapped his hands. "You do see. I knew you would."

"And somewhere my own mother is alive and well, and loves me as a mother should."

Crane nods excitedly. "And somewhere there is no illness, and no need for doctors."

Morgan paused before speaking. "And somewhere I am whole."

"You are whole here, Morgan." Crane shook his head.

For a moment, in this passing gesture, weary with affection, exasperated at the other man's stubbornness and refusal to understand, Morgan saw David before him, the man David might have become. "Have you learned nothing from all this?"

# ACKNOWLEDGEMENTS

I'd like to thank my usual group of readers, family and friends, in particular Lawrence Pedersen, for their patience, availability, occasional misgiving and constant critical insight. I'd like to thank my friend and agent, Isobel Dixon, for being so true in both these roles. I'd like to thank John Glynn for his skill, enthusiasm and commitment to this book, and Nan Graham, for asking the right question at exactly the right time. I'd like to thank Christian Boltanski, one of whose works showed me the way forward when I thought I might be lost. And, as always, for everything else, I'd like to thank Giuseppe.